THE
FLEA
THING

THE
FLEA
THING

BRIAN FALKNER

WALKER BOOKS
AND SUBSIDIARIES

LONDON • BOSTON • SYDNEY • AUCKLAND

This edition published in 2007 by
by Walker Books Australia Pty Ltd
Level 2, 1 – 15 Wilson Street,
Newtown, NSW 2042 Australia
www.walkerbooks.com.au

First published in 2003 by
Mallinson Rendel Publishers Limited
PO Box 9409, Wellington, New Zealand

National Library of Australia Cataloguing-in-Publication Entry:

Falkner, Brian.
The flea thing.

For primary school aged children.
ISBN 978 1 921150 12 8.
ISBN 1 921150 12 2.

1. New Zealand Warriors (Football team) - Juvenile fiction.
2. Rugby League football - New Zealand - Juvenile fiction.
3. Space and time - Juvenile fiction. 4. Friendship -
Juvenile fiction. I. Title.

NZ823.3

Typeset in Minion Regular by Kirby Jones
Printed and bound in China

10 9 8 7 6 5 4 3 2 1

For my dad,
who always has the time.

CONTENTS

ONE

HEADS I WIN, TAILS I WIN TOO!

'I want to be a Warrior.' I looked straight at the large, balding man sitting behind the desk, as if daring him to laugh. He didn't. But he didn't understand either.

'That's wonderful, Danny,' he said. 'It's good to have a goal. Not many kids nowadays have something to set their sights on, and if you practise very …'

'I'm sorry to interrupt,' I said, 'cos it is rude to interrupt adults when they are talking, but I was afraid that Frank Rickman wouldn't let me get another word in. 'But I don't think you understand what I mean. I want to be a Warrior *now*. This season. I want to play in the NRL.' I said NRL the way the commentators do on TV, running it all together so it sounds like 'enerell'.

This time Frank did laugh, but that was OK 'cos I had been expecting him to. Frank didn't know my secret. Anyway, it wasn't a nasty, sneery kind of laugh, just a chuckly, surprised kind of laugh. I carried on quickly. 'I know it sounds strange. I know I'd be the youngest-ever player in the

NRL, but I'd be the best young player you ever had. I play rugby league at school and I'm really good, and I'm really, really, really fast.'

Frank stopped chuckling and looked at me, but the chuckle was still there in his eyes. He was a huge bear of a man, a little bit plump now, but he still had most of the muscle that had made him a terrifying front rower when he used to play. He was the coach of the New Zealand Warriors and was very good at the job, although, of course, the team had never won the premiership. Frank picked up a pencil from his desk and started sharpening it with a small, metal pencil sharpener that he pulled out from a drawer. I had a pencil sharpener like that last year at school, but I lost it.

'How old are you, Danny?'

'I'll be thirteen in February. And would you mind very much calling me Daniel? I don't like Danny because ... I just don't like Danny.'

'I think you're serious, Daniel, and a serious question deserves a serious answer. But the answer is no. No, I can't put you in the squad. I can't even let you try out. You're much too young. I don't want to discourage you, and I hope you will be a Warrior one day. But not this year. Not at twelve.'

He put the pencil and the sharpener down. I smiled. I wasn't upset with his answer. I'd been expecting it, waiting for it. Frank still didn't know my secret.

I said, 'I thought you'd say no. But there's something you don't know. If you knew it, this thing, you'd put me in the team. If you put me in the team, you'd win the premiership this season. There's something very important that you don't know.'

Frank looked at me carefully. That was one of the good things about Frank, I found out later. He listened well, he thought carefully about what was said, and he always took people seriously. After a while he said, 'I can't imagine anything that would make me want to put you in the team, whether I knew it or not.' Then, because that sounded like an insult, he added quickly, 'Just because of your age, you understand. You could get very badly hurt.'

I said nothing. I just looked at Frank and kept my mouth tightly shut. Frank looked back at me. After a long moment Frank laughed again, but this was a different kind of laugh altogether. It was a huge, chesty laugh that made his belly wobble. It was the sort of laugh a bear would make if bears could laugh. Maybe they can laugh, I'm not really sure.

Frank said, 'There's more to you than meets the eye. It's hard to believe you're only twelve. OK, OK, I give up. I want to know. What is this thing that I don't know?'

I smiled again, 'cos that's what I'd been waiting for. 'I'll make you a bet.' I pointed to the pencil sharpener that was sitting just in front of Frank. 'You grab that sharpener. I'll try and beat you to it. If I win, you give me a try-out for the team. If you win, I'll go home and keep practising till I'm "old enough" to play.' That sounded a long way away!

Frank looked at me some more. I folded my arms. It was quite a big desk. The sharpener was just in front of Frank.

I'd have to get out of my chair and reach right across the desk to get to it. It wasn't a fair contest.

'You think you're pretty quick, don't you?' Frank said slowly. 'That's good. Are you as quick as Ricky Albany?' Ricky 'Road Runner' Albany was one of the Warriors' star wingers and everyone said he was one of the fastest players ever.

'Quicker,' I said, keeping my face really still, although I blinked a couple of times.

'You'd need to be very fast to outrun Ricky. He could have been a world-class sprinter if he hadn't …' In the middle of his sentence Frank suddenly slammed his hand down on top of the sharpener. '… taken up league instead.'

He looked sadly at me. At the brave twelve-year-old with the messy black hair and freckles, sitting in the big chair opposite him. He said, 'I know what you're going to say. You're going to say I cheated. But I didn't. I surprised you, and that's a very important part of the game. Don't do what the opposition expects you to do. You'll learn that as you get older.'

I blinked slowly. Twice. I smiled a small, secret smile to myself, (I didn't need to get a day older to learn that lesson). I looked up at the big man and said, 'Lift up your hand.'

Frank raised a big, grizzly bear eyebrow. Then his other eyebrow followed as I opened up my hand to show him the pencil sharpener. Frank snatched his hand away from the desk as if it was burning hot. The desk was empty.

I grinned. Frank leaned back in his chair, so far that I was afraid it was going to fall over backwards. He folded his arms, thinking about what had just happened.

12

'That's a pretty good magic trick you just showed me. How did you do it?'

'It wasn't a trick. I told you I was fast. Do I get my try-out? We had a deal.'

'Sorry, Danny, Daniel.' Frank was just a little bit thrown. 'Magic tricks won't get you into the team. Anyway, I never accepted your bet.'

'You accepted my bet the moment you banged your hand down on the desk,' I said simply. 'Even if you didn't say so.'

Frank sat forward. The suggestion of cheating brought a quick response. I just prayed it would be the right response.

'You're right, Daniel, I'm sorry. And you are far too clever for a twelve-year-old. But I still think it was a magic trick. Do it again and I'll see if I can spot how you do it.'

I put the sharpener back on the desk. 'If I get the sharpener, do I get the try-out?'

'We're not going to use the sharpener this time; we'll use a coin. My coin.' Frank looked carefully at me to see if there would be a reaction. I kept my face blank.

'That's fine. Shall we make it harder this time?'

'Harder!?'

'You put the coin in the palm of your hand. When you're ready, just close your hand and grab the coin. Where would you like me to stand?'

Frank said, with one of those funny grown-ups' smiles, 'Outside?'

I shook my head. 'I'll just stay in my chair then.'

Frank rummaged in his pocket and produced a twenty cent coin. He placed it in the centre of his palm, just below the big fleshy bump at the base of his thumb. He nodded.

'Do I get my try-out?' I asked.

'If you can snatch this coin out of my hand, from where you're sitting, before I can grab it, then you win your bet. I won't reneg.'

I had never heard the word 'reneg' before, but it was easy to work out what it meant. 'OK then,' I said, 'whenever you're ready.' I blinked twice.

Frank held my gaze for a few seconds then simply closed his hand. He did it quickly, as if he was afraid that I could do what I'd said I could, and even moved his hand a bit away from me, probably without meaning to. That would have been cheating.

I sat back in my chair and flipped the coin in the air, catching it and slapping it down on my wrist. 'Heads I win. Tails … I win too!'

Frank opened his hand slowly. I could see in his eyes that he couldn't believe it. His palm was bare. 'But you didn't even move!' He protested.

'Yes, I did,' I said. 'You didn't believe me when I said I was fast.'

I said nothing more. I wanted to, but I didn't. Somehow I knew when to stop talking. Most kids don't. Frank looked at me, then smiled and shook his head.

'I wouldn't have believed it if someone had told me about it. We're giving a couple of our second graders a run with the first grade squad this Saturday. Bring your boots.'

I stood up and reached out my hand. It was totally lost in the huge paw of the big, ex-front rower.

'We're going to win the premiership this year,' I said seriously.

Frank shook his head again. 'It's a try-out, Daniel. You're not in the squad, yet.'

'We're going to win the premiership,' I said again, without a trace of humour. 'This year.'

TWO

THE BOY WITHOUT A BRAIN

Going home in the car with Dad was the first time that I actually got excited about my upcoming try-out. I had been so careful to keep my emotions under control in the coach's office and now all that excitement came fizzing out, like a can of warm soft drink that you'd dropped on the ground before you pulled the tab.

'I got a try-out!' I bubbled before I'd even closed the door.

'Fantastic,' said Dad automatically, without an exclamation mark.

'It's on Saturday.' If Dad had been more switched on he would have asked that. But Dad wasn't switched on. Most of the time he was switched right off.

'If I do well at the try-out I could win a place on the team!!' I said with two exclamation marks, to sort of make up for Dad's lack of them. It was a bit like talking to a brick. (Or as my friend Jason Kirk put it, like licking a T-bone steak – you might as well not bother for all the good it did you, or the effect it had on the steak.) I kept talking. It was the biggest

16

day of my life, so far. I had to tell someone about it. 'It's the best rugby league team in the whole country!'

'That's good, Danny,' said Dad. 'Are they big boys?'

'They're professional rugby league players, Dad. It's the New Zealand Warriors.'

'That's nice.'

'Besides, they all have three legs, two heads and live at the bottom of Lake Pupuke.' It was really hard talking to Dad when he was like this. It actually hurt a bit too, but I was used to it.

'Lake Pupuke? Really?'

'Yeah, Dad.'

'It's nice there.'

I looked out the window and decided that I was wrong. Maybe I didn't have to tell anyone about it. Not yet anyway. Wait till I got home and could ring up Jason or Tupai. Or run over next door to see Fizzer.

It wasn't really Dad's fault. Well, it was, of course, but there were reasons why he was the way he was. Everybody had their own problems to deal with and sometimes that made them act in a funny way. The sooner you knew that about people, the sooner you stopped taking it personally.

Most kids don't understand that, though. In fact, as far as I could see, a lot of grown-ups don't understand it either.

I lost myself inside my own thoughts. Dreaming of wearing the Warriors' colours and running on to the field against the Sharks, or the Bulldogs. Or even the Brisbane Broncos! The ball in hand, the try line in front of me, just one player to beat. I didn't like to dream too much, in case the dream did not come true. But it was hard not to. Not when you'd just won a try-out with the Warriors.

Jason was at Fizzer's place when we arrived home. He and Fizzer were sitting in the middle of the driveway playing *Jun Ben Hoy*. That was a Japanese game we had been taught by an exchange student who'd been in Jason and Fizzer's class for six months. It was almost the same as paper-scissors-stone, but much faster and done to a beat, with some extra bits. It was a lot of fun.

They kept playing until I got out of the car, ducked underneath the garage door as it closed, and ran over to them. I kept my face perfectly calm and, once I'd brushed through the small line of shrubs that separate the two properties, I slowed down to a walk.

Jason looked up at me. His eyebrows asked the question. Fizzer voiced it, 'How'd you go?'

'Fine, thanks,' I said in my most casual voice. 'Who's winning?'

'Come on, Daniel,' cried Jason. 'Did you or didn't you?'

'Well,' I said, drawing out the suspense as long as I could, although I knew the others had guessed by now. 'Yes. I try out on Saturday!'

Fizzer whooped with excitement and Jason high-fived me.

'The Warriors! Unbelievable!' shouted Jason.

'Bags tell Phil Domane!' said Fizzer.

'The boy without a brain!' chipped in Jason.

'No …' I started, although I would have loved to.

'Oh, you've got to, you have to,' Jason and Fizzer chorused together.

'But if I try out and don't get in, he'll be rubbing it in for weeks. Don't tell Phil.'

Phil Domane was the captain of the Glenfield Giants and was in Area 15 at our school. He was the biggest boy in the team, the biggest in his class, and he was a good rugby league player. He just wasn't very nice. Jason called him the 'boy without a brain'. Not 'cos he was thick, he wasn't, but 'cos he could never be bothered to try hard at school. Compared to Jason, who had to try twice as hard as anybody else to do half as well, it just didn't seem fair.

Phil was always hassling me. If I dropped the ball, or didn't make a tackle, I'd hear about it from Phil for days afterwards. It wasn't a very captainly way to behave, and he didn't treat the other players the same way, but he always seemed to give me lots of stick.

'Get over it, Daniel, you sad frog,' said Jason, who said things like that. 'How many twelve-year-old kids even get to try out for the Warriors? Phil is going to be spewing!'

It was true. That was the real reason I didn't want Phil to find out.

'What are you guys doing now?' asked Jason, still excited.

'Why?' I asked.

'Nothing,' answered Fizzer.

'Grab your bikes. Tupai said he'd meet us at the Lost Park. Let's cycle over there and tell him the news.'

THREE

THE BEST DEFENCE

Jason came with me on Saturday. I didn't really want him to, and I didn't really know why I didn't want him to. But Jason wanted to come and, as he pointed out, if I didn't get in the team, this might be Jason's only chance to see me having a run with the Warriors' first grade squad.

Fizzer and Tupai had wanted to come too, but our team was playing Northcote that day and they couldn't afford to lose so many players.

None of the kids in my class at school knew. They wouldn't have believed me if I'd told them. They knew I was a good player, a star even, but the Warriors were grown-ups and professionals. There was a whole universe between the Warriors and the Glenfield Giants.

But Jason was there, and before long I would be very glad that I had let Jason come. Some of the other kids at school didn't like Jason very much; they thought he was a bit slow. But I knew that was just his way of talking and that, really, Jason was one of the smartest kids in the school. I also knew that Jason didn't read or write too well, another reason that some kids thought he was stupid, but it was just a dumb disease called dyslexia. Lots of kids have it, although Jason was the only one in my class. Actually, I wasn't sure that 'disease' was the right word, but I didn't know quite what else to call it.

Jason and I were close friends. Not best friends, 'cos boys don't have 'best' friends. That's something that girls do. But Jason was a close friend, and I didn't have any friends closer. So that was kind of a best friend in a way.

My dad took us to the try-out. He didn't come to watch though. He sat in the car with his briefcase doing his GST Return, whatever that is.

I had been up since six, too excited to sleep. Then, when we were getting ready to go, I couldn't find my boots. I had started to panic for a moment, but just then there was a knock on the front door and Jason had shown up with them. He had taken them the previous day without telling me and had cleaned them carefully, every inch of them, with a toothbrush. Then he had polished them blacker than black. When I put them on at the Warriors' training ground they shone like a pair of brand new boots, not the second-hand pair from the club's 'used boots' shop that they really were. I said 'thanks' to Jason, but that didn't seem like a big enough word somehow.

Frank was putting the squad through some rigorous exercises when we arrived. There were jumps and press-ups and lots and lots and lots of wind sprints. To be honest, I didn't actually know they were called wind sprints until later. It was something that Frank had picked up from a season he had spent in the United States with a Grid Iron coach.

It all looked very difficult, and the tackling exercises looked really gruesome.

'He gobbled the dirt like a bobcat,' Jason said, after one player ended up face down on the field after a particularly hard tackle. Jason was like that. He had his own language. He would never say something was 'funny'. He'd say it was 'funny as a monkey in a three-piece suit'. As far as I knew he just made the stuff up, but he always seemed to have a phrase ready at hand.

We noticed that Ricky 'Road Runner' Albany avoided a lot of the tackling exercises. He seemed to see himself as being above all that and, I suppose, in a way he was. He was a flying winger, not a front row forward. It didn't please Frank very much, that was obvious, and a couple of times he had to bawl Ricky out to get involved.

'He's lazy,' said Jason, watching with me from the sidelines.

'He's a winger,' I said. 'He can't afford to get injured in training.'

'I couldn't give the liver of a two-ton goose,' said Jason. 'He's lazy and a scaredy-chicken.'

Henry Knight ran over near the fence we were leaning against. He started doing some stretching exercises. He was the biggest player on the team. Up close he looked three times as large as he did on the TV. If his skin had been green he would have looked like the Incredible Hulk. Henry smiled at us.

'Hi, guys. You here to watch the training?'

Jason said, 'No, we're …' but I cut him off.

'Sort of,' I said, not wanting to give too much away.

'Well, enjoy yourselves,' Henry said. 'We've got a new player coming in today to try out.'

Jason blurted out before I could stop him, 'That's him. Daniel.'

Henry stopped stretching for a moment and looked down at me from a towering height. He seemed to grow bigger as he looked, or was I suddenly shrinking? I felt about as big as a flea. Which was kind of a funny thought, 'cos nobody actually called me that till much later.

Henry said, 'No, I mean for the first graders.'

'Yeah, ya snot-gropper, it's Daniel.' Jason insisted. I kicked him, which must have hurt with the boots on, but he didn't show it. Henry laughed, a huge eruption that rumbled out from somewhere deep in the mountain that he was.

'Good on you, kid, good one.'

'It's true,' I said quietly, a little bit peeved, although I knew I shouldn't be.

There was a 'hoy' from behind him. Henry stopped laughing and looked around at Frank, who was waving his arm. 'Hoy, Daniel.'

Jason told me later that the look on Henry's face when I swung my legs over the fence and trotted over towards Frank was like he'd just been smacked in the face with a raw albatross.

'Team, I'd like you to meet Daniel,' Frank said in a big grizzly bear voice that stopped talking right across the field.

Even Ricky, who was complaining to one of the trainers about something, shut up immediately. 'Daniel is twelve. He's here to try out for the first grade squad.'

There was laughter from everybody, except for Henry, who knew a little more than the rest. Frank spoke again and the laughter stopped immediately.

'I'm not kidding. This week Daniel earned the right to try out for the team. Don't ask me how. It's highly unusual, but he's here, he means business, and I think we need to give Daniel the respect that he deserves.'

Ricky had been wandering over towards me while the coach had been talking. He stepped up to me and put out his hand. I shook it, a little bit nervously.

'Welcome, Daniel,' Ricky said with a sincere smile. 'I hope you do well.'

'Thanks.' It was hard not to be overawed in the presence of all the players I had watched so often on the television. Henry tousled my hair from behind. From anyone else, I would have been annoyed. It was the sort of thing you do to a child, not a twelve-year-old. But Henry seemed to treat everyone that way. In a way, I supposed, when you are that big, everyone else would seem like a kid.

Frank said, 'Daniel, this is a first for me. It's a first for all of us. We've never had a twelve-year-old try out before. I'm not sure what to do.'

I was quite sure what to do, but I didn't want to say so. Not just yet. So I said, 'I'll be thirteen before the season starts.'

'Yeah, coach,' said Ainsley, the little five-eighth. 'Get it right.'

There was laughter from around the field, but that was exactly what I had wanted.

'I'll make a bet with you, Mr Rickman,' I announced loudly, using the coach's surname deliberately.

Frank groaned. 'Not again!'

'Give me the ball. I'll go down that end. You put your best tacklers on the field. If I can make it to the other end and score a try, I get a place in the squad. That's all.'

There were claps and cheers from the players, but Frank looked serious. 'That's a big call,' he said, no doubt thinking about the pencil sharpener and the coin. 'You have surprised me before.'

I snapped shut the trap I had been preparing with an almost audible clang.

'Are you saying that the best tacklers, in the best rugby league team in the country, can't stop a twelve-year-old boy from scoring a try?'

The claps and cheers were louder this time. 'Yeah, *Mr Rickman*,' someone called out from the back.

'My best tacklers,' Frank said at last.

'That's right,' I said, more confidently than I felt. 'Your best defence.'

'All right, you've got a deal, unless anyone objects?' Nobody did. Frank reached down and shook my hand. 'That's what we call a Gentleman's Agreement. Sealed with a handshake. But I've got to be honest with you, Daniel. They're all my best tacklers! Get out there chaps. All of you.'

Frank tossed me a ball. The players, thirty or so in number, began to move around on the field. I, however, stood my ground.

'That's not fair. There are only thirteen players in a side. You can't put the whole squad out there, reserves and all. That's more than you'd ask of anyone trying out.'

'You're right, kid,' Frank said, and I noted that it was the first time he had called me 'kid'. It wasn't to be the last. 'But you're not just anyone. You're twelve, nearly thirteen, and if you were somehow to succeed in this, my neck would be on the block. These are not kids' games here. This is serious, professional rugby league and there's a lot of money at stake.'

He called out to the other players, spreading themselves out into a defensive pattern on the field.

'Understand this, chaps. We can only have so many players in the squad. If Daniel scores his try, then one of you will have to be dropped to make room for him. I know he's just a kid, but he's fast. Faster than you are going to believe. So take this try-out seriously. Standard sliding defence. Reserves form a second defensive line behind the run-on players. Anybody not understand me?' A chorus of grunts showed that the jovial attitude was now subdued, just a bit.

'Daniel, do your best. But remember these are top, professional players. They tackle fast and they tackle hard.

They will try not to hurt you, but they will stop you. Believe me. They will stop you.'

And that was the end of the speech. But, like a lot of endings, it was really the beginning of something else. Something else indeed.

FOUR

THE THING

From the far end of the football field the opposition goal line looked a long way away. Further than it looked when we played junior grade games at Glenfield Park. Still, I reminded myself, it was the same game. True they were bigger, a lot bigger. True, they were faster, and more skilled. But, I told myself over and over again, they were about to get the shock of their lives.

The grass was greener than at most of the grounds I played on. Better looked after, no doubt. The goalposts were higher too. We were on the second grade field, adjacent to the main stadium, but it still seemed a world away from Glenfield Park.

The top players in the squad formed an impenetrable wall that looked as high as a tree and as solid as concrete. Behind them, should I make it that far, was another wall, just as big, just as hard.

I tucked the ball under my arm and began to run. I weaved a little, angling back and forth as I approached 'the wall', probing for weaknesses: a lazy player; half a gap. There were none. I ran up almost within arm's reach of the wall, and as they moved forward to tackle me, I circled away from them, back towards my own goal line. They didn't follow me, preferring to keep their line intact.

I darted towards the left side of the field, away from the wing of the speedster, Ricky. The sliding defence slid across with me, a solid wall of jerseys. I circled away again.

Then I did the Thing. I blinked. Twice.

It was the Thing I had done in Frank's office. The Thing I did when my side was losing and needed to score. The Thing that I had been able to do ever since I could remember. In fact it had taken me quite a few years to realise that other people could not do the Thing. So I kept it quiet. Jason knew about it. My parents sort of knew about it, but didn't understand it and preferred not to talk about it. Jenny, my girlfriend, thought she knew about it, but she only knew half of it and that was all she was ever going to know. And she wasn't even my girlfriend, really.

Blinking twice wasn't the Thing. I don't even know why I blinked. I couldn't help it, it just happened when I did the Thing. I blinked twice as I did the Thing and the world turned into slow motion. Slooowwww moootttttiiionnnn. Like on the action replays on the television when the video ref is trying to work out if a player actually grounded the ball. Everything went into slow motion, except for me. I was still on normal play.

That was how I had got the pencil sharpener and the coin. If I did the Thing and then moved as fast as I could, it was so fast in the 'real world' that I was just a blur.

I ran towards Ricky's wing. I ran, but not too fast, a sort of leisurely run. If I ran as fast as I could it would look strange, like I had almost disappeared, and I didn't want to give the game away. Give my Thing away.

The Warriors' heads turned in slow motion to watch me as I streaked (in their eyes) towards the wing. Ricky was already moving to intercept me and the other players were trying to close up gaps as quickly as they could. A couple of metres from the line I stepped off my right boot and changed direction suddenly towards the left. The team were still sliding to the right as I tucked through half a gap that had appeared beside Henry, who hadn't managed to slide across as quickly as the rest.

It was as easy as that. 'I'm in the team!' I thought to myself, although I knew I wasn't there yet. I still had the second line of defence to beat. And, as so often happens, that one, quick thought, that one tiny lapse of concentration, turned out to be a big, bad mistake.

I ran a few paces towards the second line then changed course again. I changed course right into Brad Smith, who, to be honest, was doing little more than standing there wondering what the heck was going on. Brad had rushed up out of the second line, hoping to strengthen the first line. It wasn't the smartest thing to do, in fact it went against everything they trained for. But Brad wasn't the smartest, or the best player on the team, and that's what he did.

He shouldn't have been there, but he was. I should have been looking, but my eyes were in the other direction and my mind, for just a second, was on my wonderful victory-to-be. And so I ran straight into Brad. I bounced off – naturally – and ended up flat on my backside on the ground.

The ball popped up out of my arms in the collision. Brad snatched at it, missed, and knocked it straight into the arms of the fastest Warrior of all time, Ricky 'Road Runner' Albany. Ricky did what any highly trained, professional rugby league player would do. He did it instinctively. He grabbed the ball in both hands and headed for the try line. My try line!

'Score!' shouted out from half a dozen places in the team, and Ricky was well on his way to doing just that. Henry wasn't looking at Ricky. He was looking at me and his eyes were soft and sad.

Brad was looking at Ricky, and he would swear afterwards that he could not understand what happened next. Neither could Ricky, but that's a different story.

Ricky had started from nearly halfway, and he was only a couple of metres or so from the try line when I recovered enough from the bump to work out what was going on. At first I wanted to cry, but at twelve, nearly thirteen, you are far too old to cry. Then I caught a glimpse of Jason's face on the sideline.

It was funny. There I was, sitting in the middle of the paddock with the fastest Warrior alive about to score a try against me. I had missed out on the Warriors' squad, and

Jason was smiling. He wasn't smiling because it was funny, or because he was laughing at me. Jason wasn't like that. He was smiling because he still believed that I could do it.

That's what got me back to my feet. That's what got me running, sprinting. That's how I reached Ricky even as he was diving over the line for the try.

I punched the ball out of Ricky's hands. It wasn't easy, he was holding it tightly, but I had the strength of desperation, and Jason's smile. The ball came loose. It bounced, and as rugby balls often do, bounced on one end, straight back into my arms.

I spun around and streaked for the defensive line. I was halfway up the field before Ricky tried to mow the lawn with his molars (Jason's description) in the in-goal area. The line was still solid. No matter what happened they kept their defensive line intact. I headed straight for the hardest, heaviest part of the line. Henry Knight.

Henry was massive. He was one of the league's best tacklers. He was as strong as a gorilla and had over a hundred first grade games under his belt. And he was standing with his legs apart. That, to me, was like an open doorway.

I ran straight at Henry, ducked beneath his clutching arms, slid along the grass between his legs and jumped back to my feet on the other side. I dashed towards the sideline as the sliding defence slid across again. Brad and Bazza White were now guarding the wing, as Ricky was still spitting out grass in the in-goal area.

I ran straight towards them and skirted the sideline even as they reached out to grab me and 'bundle me into touch' as the TV commentators put it. Then I put the brakes on. I just stopped.

In slow motion Brad and Bazza bundled themselves into touch in front of me and suddenly there was nobody between me and the goal line.

I almost ambled down to the line, checking carefully behind me so there would be no surprises. I blinked out of the Thing and placed the ball on the black dot between the posts. I looked up, for some reason expecting a roar from the crowd, but there was just a shocked silence. It seemed to last forever.

In the distance, Jason was jumping up and down by the fence; I'd never seen him so excited. Frank was striding on to the field. He looked at me and his voice was calm, although his eyes did not seem happy.

'I could get fired for this,' he said evenly, 'and I don't know how you're going to fit it in with your schoolwork, but I don't reneg on a deal. You're on the team.'

The other players looked around at each other in amazement, except for Ricky, who stalked past me without a word.

'Brad,' Frank said carefully, motioning with his arm. 'Come for a walk with me. I need to talk to you.'

FIVE

THE LOST PARK

At the end of Manuka Park, not far from the new playground, is the Lost Park. Nobody knows it's there, except for me, and Jason, Fizzer and Tupai. And this old guy who wears faded, grey track pants and a white sunhat pulled down over his eyes, and jogs, more of a totter really, back and forth, back and forth, hour after hour, every Sunday afternoon.

We were on our way to the Lost Park. It was a Friday. Friday the 13th, Black Friday. That didn't worry us, in fact we thought it was kind of cool. If we'd seen a black cat we would have chased it under a ladder. It was Friday, and that meant that I'd been a Warrior for six days now. Of course, nobody knew outside of the team and my close mates, and I hadn't actually trained with the team, let alone played a game for them, so I wasn't really a Warrior yet. But I felt like one.

I had kept it quiet partly because I don't like to make a big noise about these things, and partly because Frank had asked me to. Something about 'handling the media', which

I think meant he was worried about how the newspapers and the public were going to take the news.

So I hadn't told anyone, and I especially hadn't told Phil Domane, the boy without a brain. Although I nearly let the cat out of the bag when we ran into him on our way to the Lost Park that Black Friday.

We were going down for a kick around. Tupai and Fizzer were tossing the ball back and forth between their bikes, which is quite hard to do really, but they were good at it. Jason and I chatted as we cycled along behind.

Fizzer's real name is Fraser, but everyone called him Fizzer because he had this really extraordinary talent. Some kids were good at sports, and other kids were good at music, and other kids could balance spoons on their noses or make farting sounds with their armpits. Fizzer could taste the difference between different kinds of soft drink.

He could tell Coca-Cola from Pepsi (although everyone could do that). But Fizzer could tell diet coke from normal coke. He could tell coke out of a can from coke out of a bottle. He could even tell the difference between coke from a two-litre bottle and coke from a 1.25 litre bottle, as long as it was fresh.

It was an extraordinary talent, and also extraordinarily useless. What good is it, everyone said, to be a cola-connoisseur? Of course Fizzer proved them all wrong a couple of years later. But that's a different story.

We parked our bikes in the big, grey, old-fashioned bike stand down at the boat ramp and chained them all together.

We walked up into Manuka Park but had to wait there a while. Phil was chucking a Frisbee around with Emilio and Blocker, two of his mates. We didn't want him to see us going into the Lost Park.

'Getting in some practice, Danny boy?' Phil sneered at me. 'Just as well, you need it.' I ignored him and we walked past. I don't know why he had to be nasty all the time. Everybody had their own problems, I knew that, but I couldn't see what Phil's was. Jason gave him a Crazy Jason glare. That was when he did this thing with his eyes that made him look like a psychopathic axe murderer. It freaked most people out but Phil just ignored it.

'I heard they're starting a girl's league next year at Glenfield. Maybe they'll let you join.'

I bit my lip and kept walking. No point in getting into a slanging match with a moron.

'Or maybe you'll just go back to ballet school.'

That last quip was unfair. My mum had made me take up ballet three years earlier. I had stuck with it for a whole year. It actually wasn't all that bad, but it was pretty tough on a kid from Glenfield to be taking ballet lessons and I had screamed and fought the next year not to go back. But the remark still stung and I just couldn't help snapping back.

'Keep talking, Junior Grader,' I said with a mean smirk, 'I'm going to play for the Warriors.'

It was supposed to be a comeback, a put-down, but it didn't work like that.

'You! A Warrior!?' Phil could hardly choke the words out, he was laughing so much, and his mates were laughing with him. 'Keep dreaming!'

'No …' Fizzer started, but I shot him a shut-up glance. I had already said too much. Jason was looking a little hurt. Then it struck me that my friends were also Junior Graders. If I had put Phil down, I had put them down too. I can be really stupid like that sometimes.

'The day you run on for the Warriors, I'll fart the National Anthem before the game!' Phil was really enjoying himself.

Tupai said, 'Come on, leave these snotrags alone, let's go kick the ball around.'

Phil glared at being called a snotrag, but there was nothing he could do about it. He wasn't brave enough to take on Tupai. Tupai was the strongest kid in the school. He had once broken a fifty cent piece in half in his bare hands. Or so the story went. Really Fizzer and I had cut it in half in metalwork class and glued it back together with craft glue. It snapped really easily, but Tupai already had a reputation by that stage and the fifty cent piece just added a little more colour to the legend.

'Come on, guys, we'll leave the ballerina and his friends to their ballet practice.' Phil tossed the Frisbee at Blocker and the three of them sauntered off, shirts untucked, hands in pockets.

I shook off Phil with a short shake of my head and, as soon as he was out of sight, we ducked into the secret track.

Manuka Park stretches from the boat ramp at the end of the road, all the way up to Kyle Bush. In the middle, in the flat bit, is where they built the playground, a yellow and red plastic thing that nobody plays on except for the young kids. It's OK, I suppose. I mean it has swings and some short, curving slides, and this kind of overhead seesaw thing, but it's all a bit, well, not dangerous enough for most of the kids I know. 'Tame' might be the right word for it.

If you go past the playground and head straight up the hill, keeping the big seesaw thing in line with the lone pine on the other side of the boat ramp, you come to the track that leads to the Lost Park. I don't know when it got lost, but I know when it got found. That was about a year ago, maybe a bit longer, when Tupai, Jason, Fizzer and I were practising goal kicking in Manuka Park.

It was Tupai's turn, and, although he wasn't the most accurate kicker, boy did he have a mean boot on him. He lined up, took three paces backwards and one to the side, jiggled his hands like Andrew Merhtens, which always made us laugh, and launched himself at the ball.

Jason reckoned that the ball shivered when it saw him coming, and I wouldn't blame it if it did. Like I said, Tupai had a real mean boot on him. Anyway, the ball sagged to the side and Tupai caught it on the outside of his boot and the ball went flying up the hill into Kyle's bush. Right in line with the seesaw thing and the lone pine by the boat ramp.

Tupai shrugged and went off up the hill to get it, and

when he hadn't come back a few minutes later, we all went up to help him look for it.

He was just standing there with the ball tucked under one arm. 'Look at this,' he'd said. So we looked. The ball had landed on a couple of concrete steps. But what were steps doing in the middle of the bush? We figured that if there were steps, they must have been part of a path, and if there was a path, then it must have led somewhere. So we kind of crashed through the bush in the direction the steps were pointing.

We pushed our way down a small gully to a creek and, to our immense surprise, over the creek there was an old, wooden, and mostly rotten bridge. The track was more clearly formed on the other side of the creek, the bush hadn't reclaimed it quite as badly. The track led over a small ridge and out into what we now call the Lost Park.

It's an amazing place, the Lost Park, and it's our secret. Jason called it the Park that Time Forgot, although I think really it is the park that the City Council forgot. I can only guess at what happened. Once upon a time Manuka Park must have been a much bigger park with a bush section in the middle, joined by the track. Maybe one year the entrance to the track got a bit overgrown and the council workers missed it when they were cutting back weeds and stuff. Then, over the years, it got completely overgrown and disused.

It's quite big, the lost park, about half the size of a footie field, but not that shape. It has no shape really, just like a big ink blot. In the park is a playground, but it's a playground like none you've ever seen anywhere else. It's a playground from the days before they started making everything out of red and yellow plastic with rubberised landing mats in case you fall off.

There's this fort thing, a huge wooden structure with three different levels. There are ladders and firemen's poles to take you from one level to the next, and a drawbridge that you can actually raise from inside the fort to keep out any enemies. Just along from the fort is the tractor. A real tractor! Not a working one, the engine is just a big block of rust and the tyres are filled with concrete, but it's a real tractor that had once hauled hay around some farm somewhere.

But the pride and joy of the park is further along again, mounted on the crest of a small bump in the ground. The Spitfire. We all called it the Spitfire. It isn't, it's a Hawker Hurricane. I know because I looked it up on the Internet. But when we first found it we called it the Spitfire and the name kind of stuck. It's a real airplane. Maybe it had really flown in the Battle of Britain. It had been mounted on a circle of concrete and its skin had been replaced with aluminum. A hole had been cut in the bottom of the cockpit so you could climb into it and pretend you were flying. It was the best thing.

I guess that this is what parks were like when my dad was a kid. Not tame at all. In fact I'm sure it was downright dangerous. We loved it.

We kicked the ball around and practised passing for a while, just for fun. Then Fizzer wanted to take on Tupai in a wrist-wrestling match to see if he could beat him. We all knew he couldn't, Tupai was the strongest kid in the school, and possibly the world, but Fizzer had been secretly practising for weeks with a machine he'd built out of some bits of wood and rubber from an old inner tube. We knew he couldn't beat Tupai though. Nobody could beat Tupai in a wrist-wrestle, so Jason and I went to play in the Spitfire.

I climbed up first and got the Messerschmitt out. I had found a picture on the Internet of a Messerschmitt 109 and printed it on my dad's printer. Jason had stuck it to a bit of wood and cut it out with the jigsaw in woodworking class. Then he had mounted it on an old-broom handle.

I handed the Messerschmitt down to Jason and sat in the rusty old seat. I grasped the joystick and shouted 'Chocks away!' It is amazing how much your imagination can fill in if you give it a head start. The rusting old cockpit of the plane lost its age and funny, old, brown colour. It grew shiny and new before my eyes. The green grass of the park all around turned to fluffy, white cumulus clouds, and suddenly I was soaring, the motor screaming dangerously as I climbed into the sun, scanning the horizon for any sign of the Heinkel bomber fleet the radar had picked up.

I levelled off and cruised in a south-easterly direction. If they were heading for London I should intercept them on that heading … Messerschmitt! Where had he come from? A sleek and deadly 109 angling in from five o'clock. They were fast, the 109s. Not as fast as a Spitfire though, and not as manoeuvrable as my trusty Hurricane. I flung the plane to the left and pulled it into a circle, but Jerry stuck to me like glue. I barrel-rolled and dived, then flipped over into a hard figure eight that I knew he couldn't match. There he was, three o'clock, diving for the ground. I dropped my right wing and banked hard on to his tail.

Rat-a-tat-a-tat, a plume of smoke and the dive became a plunge. I followed him long enough to see the crash in an empty paddock, then pulled up, waving to the farmhands cheering in the fields below.

'Daniel,' Jason said. 'Gizza go.'

'Yeah, sure,' I said. 'Your turn.'

I ran around with the Messerschmitt for him for a while, then both of us joined Fizzer and Tupai who were lying on their backs on the long grass trying to find shapes in the clouds.

'Who won?' I asked, just to be polite.

'Tupai,' Fizzer said. 'But I nearly had him this time.'

I looked at Tupai, who smiled.

Fizzer asked, 'Do you reckon that one looks like Santa Claus?'

I couldn't see it, so I said nothing, but Jason nodded and Tupai said, 'Absolutely.'

Jason burst out laughing.

'What?' asked Fizzer.

'Absolutely,' Jason said. 'That's not a real word. That's one of those words grown-ups use when they don't want to say no. Like, "Dad, can we go to Disneyland for our next holidays?" "Sure son. Absolutely." But you never do.'

Then Jason said, quite out of the blue it seemed, 'It'll be a shame not having you around.'

I looked at him, to make sure he was talking about me, which he was.

'Don't be such a spoon,' I said quickly. 'I'll be around just as much.'

'How do you reckon that?' asked Jason. 'You'll have training. A lot of training. And when the season starts you'll be playing every weekend.'

'I'll be around,' I said. 'You'll hardly notice I'm gone.'

I kind of believed it when I said it, but I was wrong of course. Tragically wrong.

SIX

TRAIN LIKE THE WIND

My first day of training with the New Zealand Warriors was almost my last day of training with the New Zealand Warriors, but big Henry Knight saved my life.

Training, for me at least, was every day after school from four till seven. Dad took me to training that first day, leaving Mum in charge of the small art gallery they ran together. He didn't come to watch, just sat in the car doing something called 'inventory' and 'stock lists'. That was his way, I guess, of making use of the time.

Training was hard. Harder than I would have believed, and even though Frank made certain allowances for me because of my age, it was still tough going.

There were wind-sprints. That's a ten metre dash across to a marked line, touch the ground, then a ten metre dash back to where you started from, touch the ground, dash back to the line, and so on. We did lots of wind-sprints.

We did wind-sprints and push-ups, and wind-sprints and

star-jumps, and wind-sprints and weight-training. Did I mention wind-sprints? We did a lot of those!

A good part of the training session, just when we were exhausted from all the wind-sprints, was combinations. That's where Frank would line up two teams on the field, one defensive and one attacking, and try out various attacking combinations against various defensive combinations. Combinations are set moves, planned in advance, that are supposed to open up holes in the opposition's defensive line. All teams do them. In a way they are like little dances where everybody knows what they are going to do next. So maybe rugby league does have something in common with ballet after all. Just don't tell Phil Domane!

We all did a lot of broken play training. Broken play is where things haven't gone to plan for one team or the other and the attacking and defensive lines are all at odds and ends. Some players are terrified of broken play, others thrive on it. I loved it. I loved it at the Glenfield Giants, and I loved it at the Warriors.

Players all over the park and the ball loose on the ground. I'd scoop it up one-handed and almost always score a try. I ran around them, I ran through them, if they fell over I ran over them. I even ran under them if their legs were apart, like Henry on that first day.

Dad's car was parked right alongside the training ground and once, after I had scored a training try, he looked up, and I thought he had noticed. But he just frowned and looked back at his books. Henry noticed. He was patting me on the back for the try and he saw where I was looking and, I guess, he saw the hopeful, then disappointed expression on my face.

'What's wrong with your dad?' Henry asked.

'Oh, nothing,' I said, more cheerfully than I felt. 'He's just really busy and I guess it's a pain to give up three hours every evening.'

'Why does he stay if he's not going to watch?'

'Well, we live all the way over in Glenfield, and it takes about forty minutes to get here. So, if he dropped me off and came to pick me up later, he'd spend most of the time driving.'

Henry nodded.

I continued, 'He's not really a rugby guy, anyway. Dad and Mum are more into arty things. Mum used to be a dancer and they run a small art gallery.'

'Cut the chatter, kid!' Frank called from the sideline. Henry winked at me and ran back into position. More broken play. The ball bounced in front of Ainsley, who tried to toe it forward but he missed it and just knocked it sideways. It skittered along the ground a way, just out of Fuller's reach, and ended up in front of me again. I picked it up, side-stepped Brownie who was charging in for a tackle, and bounced and hopped my way down to the try line for another try.

Frank was shaking his head and clapping his hands slowly at the same time. I'm not sure what that meant, but I guess it was good.

'He's like a little flea, hopping all over the place,' Michaels said with exasperation. I'd ducked and weaved around him not once but twice on my way to the goal line. Most of the players laughed. Ricky glared at me.

'Come over here, Flea,' Frank called, and they all laughed. The name was mine from then on. 'OK,' Frank continued, 'you can attack. But what on earth are you going to do when you've got someone like Henry charging at full steam towards you and you're the only person between him and the try line? You've got to be able to defend if you want to get on the field, and I just don't see how you can do it.'

There was a bit of a silence as I thought about this. I'd been thinking about it a lot, and I had a few ideas, but I knew they were about to be tested.

'In judo,' I said eventually, 'they teach you to use your opponent's strength against him.'

Frank nodded. 'I practised judo for more than ten years, I know the ...' He stopped suddenly and looked at me strangely. 'But you already knew that, didn't you?'

I smiled. I did know that. I had read Frank's autobiography.

'Yes,' Frank continued, 'you already knew that. Don't try to be too clever with me, kid. I may be an old front rower but I've still got a few brain cells left. Now tell me how a flea is going to stop a charging elephant.'

Henry made a noise like an elephant trumpeting, and everybody laughed. Frank threw him the ball. 'Henry, squash the Flea for me.' He smiled at me though, so I knew he wasn't angry with me.

The other players cleared off the field and Henry went up to halfway and stood there for a moment tossing the ball from one massive hand to the other massive hand. Then he began to trot, then to run, then to charge. It looked like a freight train was coming at me without brakes.

I stood my ground right in front of him, but when he was nearly about to roll over me like a steamroller he suddenly broke stride and pulled to a halt.

'I can't do this, coach,' he said. 'He really will get squashed.'

Frank looked at me. 'Flea, it's your call. Do you want to do this?'

I looked Henry straight in the eye as I said, 'You bet.' Then I said quietly so only Henry could hear me, 'Don't chicken out this time.'

Henry shook his head and trotted back to halfway. Then he came at me again. Forget the freight train, this time he was an asteroid on a collision course with earth.

Once again I held my ground, right in front of him and at the last moment feinted into a tackle. Henry prepared for the impact, but I was doing the Thing and I had no intention of tackling a monster like Henry head on. I skipped to one side and ankle-tapped him from behind as he ran past. Ankle-tapping is easy if you're in the right position, you just push one of their ankles to the side so that it hits their other ankle as they try to run. If you've ever tried to run with your shoelaces tied together, that's pretty much the same thing. Your body keeps going forward but your legs stay still.

The bigger they are, the harder they fall, as the saying goes, and Henry hit the ground hard. He had the ball tightly tucked under one wing, but there's an enormous jolt when you hit the ground at speed and, at that moment, the ball is as loose as it will ever be, no matter who is carrying it. Henry didn't lose the ball, well, not by himself. I just ran up alongside as the behemoth began to topple and just as he hit the ground I nudged the ball out with my toe.

I blinked out of the Thing, ran across to Frank and tossed him the ball. He was laughing. On the field Henry was sitting up and laughing also.

'One day you'll cease to amaze me,' Frank said, 'but this is not the day. Get changed, all of you. That's enough for today.'

Ricky 'Road Runner' Albany was the only player who didn't congratulate me as we walked back to the changing sheds, and after showers he took off without a word. As Henry walked with me over to Dad's car, I wondered if I had done something to annoy him.

Dad was standing by the driver's door looking at his watch. 'We need to talk about this,' he said, even before we got to the car.

'Hello, Mr Scott.' Henry held out a huge paw. 'I'm Henry Knight, one of Flea … Daniel's team-mates.'

Henry Knight just called me a team-mate. I grew about ten centimetres on the spot!

'Pleased to meet you, Henry,' Dad said, although clearly he wasn't.

'Is there a problem with Daniel coming to training?'

Henry towered above Dad, who looked up a little nervously. 'It's his homework. He's still at school and he can't spend so much time each week at training.'

It wasn't that at all as I knew, so did Henry, and so, I think, did Dad. He just didn't want to give up four hours each day and I could understand that.

Dad said, 'I'll have to talk to your coach. Maybe you can try out again another year.'

It was so unfair. I had already made arrangements for my homework. I was going to do some of it when I got home from training, and some in my lunch hour at school. It was nothing to do with homework.

I couldn't speak. I just stood there, in some kind of shock. My career with the Warriors was going to be over before it had got started. But that's when Henry waded in and Dad couldn't argue with what he said. Henry saved my life.

'Mr Scott, I'm sure Daniel can find time to fit in his homework. Every kid has homework, lots of them don't do it at all. I'm sure Daniel will do all of his. I know it must be difficult for you, though, to take time away from your work to bring Daniel all this way.'

Dad kind of stuttered, 'Yes, well, there is that too.'

'But I live in Dairy Flat. I drive past Glenfield every day to get to training. It would be no problem for me to pick up

Daniel on my way through and bring him home afterwards.'

'Yes, but ...'

'This is a once-in-a-lifetime opportunity for Daniel. No other kid his age has ever played for the Warriors. Anything I can do to help him realise his dream, I'd be happy to do.'

Here was Henry, an almost complete stranger, saying he'd do anything to help me, while my own father was more worried about his own problems. Even I felt guilty on my Dad's behalf.

Dad looked up at Henry for a little while. 'I guess that'd be OK,' he said finally, 'but if his homework slips I may change my mind.'

'It won't slip!' I almost shouted it with relief, but controlled my voice just in time. 'And thanks, Henry.'

'No problem, Flea,' he said with a grin, 'see you tomorrow.'

SEVEN

MASHED POTATOES

Mum invited Henry over for dinner the next week. It was a Sunday, and training finished at four, so she invited him over to say thank you for taking me to training each time. I asked if Jason and the guys could come because I had hardly seen them all week (as Jason had predicted). Mum said it was OK to invite Jason, but she wasn't going to invite the whole rugby team. 'League team', I'd corrected her, but she'd just ignored me.

To my surprise Jenny was there too. I didn't know she was coming and, to be honest, I would have been happier if Fizzer or Tupai had been there instead, what with Henry Knight there. Mum knows Jenny's mum really well and they both thought it was kind of cute that she was my girlfriend, so I guess Mum must have invited her over and forgotten to tell me.

I wasn't really sure that she was my girlfriend. We liked each other a lot and she told everyone I was her boyfriend. We'd known each other since forever and her birthday was just two weeks after mine, so we always went to each other's parties. Sometimes we held hands walking home after school, but we hadn't kissed or anything. She seemed more like a close cousin to me. Jenny coming to dinner meant I'd have to tell her about the Warriors, but that was no problem. I knew she'd keep it quiet for me. She was a good sort, Jenny.

Mum made a beautiful meal. She always did. Just like in a flash restaurant, with big white plates. This time we had what she called 'an arrangement of braised chicken breasts and vegetables on a potato croquette', with a creamy sauce drizzled across the food and the plate.

Mum liked making dinners like that when her arty friends came over, but I was a bit afraid that it would be lost on big Henry.

'This looks beautiful, Mrs Scott,' he said when she brought it out. It seemed funny him calling her Mrs Scott when he was twice her size, and Mum must have thought so too because she said, 'It's Lauren, and thank you.'

Dad was late because he had an important client visiting the gallery, so we started without him.

I carefully cut a bite-sized portion from the meat, the way I had been taught. Jenny and Jason, who had been around for dinner often enough, did the same. Jason had the most delicate table manners of anyone I knew, yet he could barely write his own name. Funny how life works like that.

'It is beautiful, Mrs Scott … Lauren,' Henry said with a smile as wide as Texas. 'The chicken is delicious.'

'Thank you, Henry.' Mum smiled.

Henry had a slightly different way of eating than the rest of us, and I struggled to hold back a laugh. He didn't cut the meat so much as stab it to death with his knife while he ripped a huge chunk off with his fork. He spun it around in the sauce before jamming the whole thing into his mouth.

'Delicious,' he said again with his mouth full. 'And so are the vegies and this um …'

'Croquette,' my mum said with a look of apprehension. 'It's a potato croquette.'

Henry looked a little confused, so I chipped in, 'It's like mashed potato baked into a shape.'

'I love mashed potato.' Henry promptly squashed the croquette flat with his fork. He mashed some of the vegies and mixed them with the potato, swirling them around in a kaleidoscope of colours on his plate.

Jason covered his face with his hand to stifle a laugh and I took a big mouthful of chicken. We weren't laughing at Henry, though. It was just that he was doing what the rest of us would have loved to do. Henry just mashed and mixed and 'manners' were not something he even thought about.

I decided then and there that I liked Henry a lot. I wanted to be like him when I was older. Laid back, easygoing, just enjoying life without following all its little rules.

Jenny asked, 'Do you play rugby too?'

'League,' said Jason, and Jenny rolled her eyes. To her rugby was rugby was rugby.

'I play for the Warriors,' said Henry, 'like Daniel.'

Jenny stopped eating. 'What do you mean? Which Warriors?'

'The New Zealand Warriors.'

'The ones on telly?'

Henry laughed. 'Yeah, those ones.'

Jenny thought about it for a minute. 'But what do you mean 'like Daniel'? He doesn't play for the Warriors. He plays for Glenfield.'

Henry looked at me.

'Not any more,' I said proudly. After all these days of keeping it a secret it felt great to be able to tell someone. 'I tried out for the Warriors and got in the first grade squad.'

Jenny actually dropped her fork. 'You mean you're going to be on telly?' She didn't really care about the rugby league, but she did care that her sort-of-boyfriend was going to be on telly.

'You can't tell anyone!' I said quickly. 'It's all under wraps until Frank – the coach – makes an announcement to the newspapers and stuff.'

Jenny looked at me out of the corner of her eye. 'Are you joking me, because I …'

Henry said, 'He's not joking. But please don't tell anyone just yet.'

'You're going to be on telly!' Jenny almost screamed it. I'd never seen her so excited. 'Oh my goodness!'

'Do they really show some of your games on television?' Mum asked, revealing the great depths of her rugby league knowledge.

'All of them,' Henry nodded.

'You never said you were going to be on television.' Mum was so surprised that she forgot her own manners and actually frowned at Henry stirring his food with his fork.

Henry froze. He glanced at me looking for all the world like a little boy who had just said a swear word in Sunday School and didn't know why he was in trouble. My heart dropped. Jason saw it too.

Jason said, 'Mrs Scott, your son's going to be famous.' And at the same time he said it he squashed his croquette flat and started stirring it into his vegetables.

Smash! My croquette followed. I winked at Henry and stirred away cheerfully. He immediately relaxed.

'Jenny, promise not to tell anyone,' I said. 'Especially not Phil Domane.'

'The boy without a brain,' said Jason.

Jenny was in Phil's class at school.

'Phil Domane, the boy without a brain!' Henry made a funny, laughing sound that I think you call a guffaw. 'Who is Phil Domane, the boy without a brain?'

'Captain of the Giants,' I said. 'He doesn't like me very much.'

'You're going to be on telly,' Jenny said again. 'You're going to be famous!'

EIGHT

JENNY CHANGES EVERYTHING

Jenny had a joke for me. It was a kids' joke, and I'd heard it before, but I played along anyway to be polite. We were walking down to the boat ramp to watch the sun set over the upper harbour. There were thick, puffy clouds scudding along the horizon and a beautiful sunset was looming.

Jenny was carrying the lifejackets and paddles and I had Dad's two-man kayak slung over my shoulder. (It was fibreglass and quite light.)

'Will you remember me tomorrow?' Jenny's joke began.

'Yes,' I replied, with just a small smile because I already knew the punchline.

'Will you remember me next week?'

'Yes.'

'Will you remember me next year?' Jenny didn't look at me, she just kept her eyes on the footpath.

'Of course I will.'

'Knock knock,' Jenny said.

'Who's there?'

'Daniel!' she said indignantly, 'you've forgotten me already.'

I laughed, even though I'd heard it before, and after a while Jenny did too. For just a moment I had the feeling that there was something more to the joke than I'd realised.

Jenny has a great laugh. Not a silly girls' giggle, and not a snorty boys' snicker. She has a wicked chuckle, a smile to match, and long auburn hair. She looks a lot like her mum, really.

I said, because it suddenly occurred to me, 'You're going to be very pretty when you're grown up.'

Jenny looked at me and chuckled her wicked chuckle. I blushed and stumbled, 'I mean, it's not that you're not pretty now, but … you're … I mean …'

Jenny said, 'I know what you mean,' and I knew she did, 'and thank you.'

It wasn't easy saying nice things to girls. Even someone like Jenny who you've known your whole life. I shut my mouth in case any more silly stuff came out of it and hoisted the kayak a bit higher on my shoulder for comfort.

Dad had bought the kayak about four or five years ago. He'd said it would give us an activity that we could do together, and it was a healthy, outdoors kind of activity, which was really good for someone like him who was stuck inside all day.

The problem was, apart from that first summer, Dad had never had the time to go kayaking with me. So he'd stayed stuck inside all day while I went kayaking with Jason, or Fizzer, or Tupai. And sometimes with Jenny.

The tide was high, which was good, because this inlet of the upper harbour was not much more than a big creek really and it was pretty rank and boggy when the tide was out. But the tide was in and the water was still and the thick native bush that surrounds the inlet was glowing softly in the half-light. It was a fantastic evening. We strapped on our life jackets and paddled quietly out from the shore.

'Is the boat still there?' Jenny asked.

'I think so.' I tapped her on the shoulder and pointed. Ahead, in the deeper, wider part of the inlet a launch was moored, scarcely moving in the still water. It was quite a distance away but the sleek kayak sliced through the water like me through a Warriors' pack, and we made good time over to the boat.

Its name was the *Emma-Rose*. It wasn't quite a luxury launch, but it wasn't all that bad either. It had one of those lowered platforms for scuba divers at the stern, and we both climbed up on to that. I tied the kayak up to a small bollard with a short painter.

The open, stern cabin had two bench seats that doubled as lockers. We climbed a small ladder up to a raised bridge with a comfortably padded captain's seat and an equally well-padded bench seat. We sat beside each other.

The tide must have still been coming in, as the *Emma-Rose's* bow was pointing up the harbour, right at the setting sun. I smiled at Jenny, and she smiled at me and brought out a small bag of biscuits that her mum had made.

'You won't forget me, will you?' Jenny said. 'When you're rich and famous.'

I laughed with my mouth full. 'I don't know about 'rich'. Everything I earn goes into a trust account until I'm eighteen. And as for famous …'

I stopped because Jenny was looking at me strangely. 'No, Jenny, of course I won't forget you.'

'But you'll be away all the time, travelling over to Australia, meeting other people.'

'I won't forget you,' I insisted.

Jenny nodded and turned her face to the sunset. It truly was a beautiful sunset. There was a sliver of clear sky along the horizon above the Waitakere mountain ranges. The sun slowly dropped down into that thin gap and actually lit the low clouds from underneath, bathing them in a mixture of blood red and molten gold.

Jenny said, 'I don't want to sound selfish, and I really do wish you all the best with your new team, but I'm worried that you'll become this big star and won't want to know us ordinary kids.'

I started to say something but Jenny put her finger to my lips to stop me. She looked back at the sun rippling off the underside of the clouds and the waters of the upper harbour.

And then she kissed me. On the lips! And that changed everything.

Well, that's not entirely true. She looked at me for a moment and the sunset caught in her eye and it was all a bit special really. Then she leaned forward to kiss me, but we were still wearing our life jackets and they got in the way, so we just kind of bounced off. I burst out laughing, then so did she.

We sat there for a moment longer, looking at each other, then Jenny unclasped her life jacket and tossed it down into the back of the boat, and after a moment I did the same. She put her hand behind my neck and kissed me gently and briefly, and it wasn't as bad as I'd thought it would be.

We just sat there as the sun slotted into the ranges in the distance. We didn't say a word, but it was a nice time anyway.

I guess after that she was no longer my sort-of-girlfriend. She was my girlfriend for real. In the future lay love and marriage and who knows what. But in the meantime, there was plenty of time just to sit. And watch the sun set.

NINE

CHAI-CHOP-SKI

'It's Tchaikovsky,' I said again, and repeated the name slowly, 'Tchaikovsky.'

'Chai-chop-ski,' Henry said for the third time, and I was starting to think he was taking the mickey. He said, 'Why do you listen to all this old stuff anyway?'

One thing my parents had instilled in me was a love of great music. Great melodies and harmonies and not just the bang-bang-scream-crash stuff that they play on the pop stations.

We were in Henry's car on the way to the first game of the season. All the weeks of training and wind-sprints now seemed just a blur. Somewhere in all the excitement and hard work I had turned thirteen, but it had been on a training day and there had been no time for a party with my friends. Henry had brought a cake along to training that day though, which was nice of him, and he'd even baked it himself, which surprised me for some reason.

It was hard to believe I was going to run on to the field at last for the New Zealand Warriors. The excitement that had been growing in me for weeks was about to erupt like a volcano, with hurtling rocks and molten lava.

I turned the stereo up a little louder and said, 'It's called the *1812 Overture* and it's about a famous battle, if you listen you can hear the French attacking, and the Russians counter-attacking.'

Henry listened for a moment or two, then jumped when we got to the part with the cannons. I had the Minneapolis Symphony Orchestra's renowned 1958 recording with the real antique French cannons.

'It's a bit like a game of league,' he said, 'all this attacking and counter-attacking.'

'It is a bit. Those are real cannons,' I said. 'Cast in France in 1775.'

'Don't you listen to any real music?' Henry asked.

'This is real music.' I was indignant.

'You know what I mean. Rock or dance music. What all the other kids listen to.'

I had listened to quite a lot of it actually but it all sounded the same to me.

'Chuck this in.' Henry handed me a CD. 'It's an oldie but a goodie.' I flipped out Tchaikovsky and put in his CD. For Henry, an 'oldie' meant something from the mid-nineties. As I expected: bang-bang-scream-crash.

'Willi One Blood. It's called *Whiney Whiney*.'

I smiled politely. It did grow on you after a while though. Henry was bouncing along in the driver's seat, banging his hands on the steering wheel. His head was nodding with the beat and he sang along to the chorus. *Man, you know what really drives me crazy*. It was kind of cool really.

'Here we are,' Henry said, pulling into the car park. 'Hey, there's your mate.'

Jason was just getting off a bus. I was looking forward to seeing him; I hadn't seen him in weeks. The entire Glenfield Giants' team was going to be there. Frank had sent the Glenfield coach a truckload of tickets, without telling him why. Even now, on the day of the first game of the season, nobody knew I was a Warrior.

Henry parked in a reserved space and I ran over to the bus to see Jason.

'Hi, Jason.'

'Hi, Daniel.' He seemed a little uncomfortable.

'How you been?'

'Good, good, you?'

'Yeah, good.' We were talking to each other like two old ladies at the local cat show.

Just then, though, Phil Domane got off the bus and I steeled myself for the usual round of insults. Blocker got off behind him.

'Danny-boy,' Phil called out. 'What are you doing here? I thought you'd given up playing league. Thought it was too hard-going for you.'

'Give it a rest, Phil,' I said.

'Oh, I forgot,' he laughed. 'I suppose you're playing for the Warriors today!' Blocker cracked up at that one but Jason just looked more and more uncomfortable.

'I suppose you'll be playing first five-eighth, replacing Ainsley Retimanu.' More laughter.

'Actually,' said a big voice from behind me, 'he'll be playing on the wing. But he's coming off the reserves' bench today.'

Phil's eyes opened wide and, for once in his life, he didn't seem to have anything to say. Behind him Blocker whispered, 'That's Henry Knight.'

I opened my mouth to ask Phil what key he was going to fart the national anthem in, but shut it again. I'd already won this round. No point in rubbing it in.

'Hi, Henry,' Jason said.

'G'day, Jason, and who's this?'

I said, 'That's Phil Domane.'

'The boy without a brain,' Henry said automatically, and I am sure he regretted it as soon as he said it. 'Oh, sorry, I didn't mean … anything.' Phil's mouth was as wide open as his eyes.

Henry wouldn't say something to hurt someone on purpose. Not even a guy like Phil Domane. It had just slipped out and I think he felt quite bad. 'Come on, Flea,' Henry said. 'Let's get into the changing room.'

I walked off with him, not saying a word. All the weeks of secrecy were suddenly worth it, just to see that look on Phil Domane's face.

I don't know how Frank had managed to keep me secret from the media for so long, but once I sat down on the reserves' bench in my Warriors' uniform I was a secret no longer. There was an endless stream of photographers snapping away at everything I did, once they realised that I was not one of the ball boys. The commentators couldn't stop going on about my age. I just felt so proud sitting down on the sideline, in my uniform, part of the greatest rugby league team in the country.

We were up against the Machetes. The Blacktown Machetes. They were a new side to the competition.

Their coach, Nathaniel Kettle, was from England and had a reputation as a hard man. As we found out during that game, and as many teams found out that season, the Machetes played hard and dirty. They played to win at all costs, and quite a few players got hurt playing against them. The worst injury that I knew of was what happened to Henry, but that didn't happen till much later in the season.

The sun shone hot over the stadium and the grandstands were almost full. That was good news for a club which had had trouble attracting good crowds in some previous years.

A tall, thin player with bright, blonde hair, his name was Carver, kicked off for the Machetes. Ainsley took the kick and fed it to Bazza who made a great run up the field but took a swinging arm from the Machetes' fullback, a mean-faced poker of a man named Dell Bean. His nickname was Rumble, I don't know why.

Bazza got up with blood pouring from his nose, but played the ball before getting help from our trainers.

The rest of the game was pretty much the same. On the Warriors' side, skill and flair, with bullocking runs from our forwards, Henry most of all. On the Machetes' side, swinging arms and elbows and every bit of rough stuff in the book, whenever they could get away with it. The referee can't be everywhere at once, and they got away with a lot.

At the end of the first half we were ahead by two points, thanks to a brilliant piece of footwork by Ricky Albany that put Ainsley into the corner on a run-around.

At the start of the second half I started looking up at the coaches' box, wondering when Frank would inject me into the game. The crowd and the commentators were all wondering the same thing, but, with just ten minutes left to play in the game, Frank had used all his other reserves and not me.

Henry burst straight through the first couple of tacklers with five minutes to go and got his arms free to feed the ball around Rumble Bean's back to Brownie, who fired a long basketball pass across to Ricky, who ran forty metres and scored the winning try with a great flourish.

A few minutes later the final whistle went and I, along with thirty thousand fans, three commentators, eighteen Warriors and most of the Glenfield Giants Rugby League Team were wondering why I hadn't got on the field.

I told myself that Frank hadn't wanted to risk me in such a tough game when we were ahead most of the time anyway. I told myself that and I hoped it was true.

I didn't even bother to have a shower afterwards. No need. I just changed and sat quietly in the corridor waiting for Henry.

'Don't worry about it,' he said when he finally emerged. 'I'm sure he'll use you next week. He'd be stupid not to.'

I smiled. 'Yeah, he'd be stupid not to.'

Henry said, 'Let's go play some Chai-chop-ski.'

TEN

MEET THE PRESS

The press conference was held in the boardroom in the Warriors' offices next door to the stadium. Usually it would have been held in the media room under the grandstand, but this was no ordinary press conference. There was me, Henry, Frank Rickman and Henshaw Walters (the Warriors' manager) all lined up at a bench table at the end of the room.

The room was long and the dark, muddy-crimson walls were lined with framed Warriors' uniforms from previous years, right back to their very first strip.

Interspersed with those were copies of newspaper articles about the team. One of them that caught my eye was a story, with a huge photograph, on the front page of the *Sydney Morning Herald*, all about Stacey Jones, the Warriors' greatest-ever player.

Behind our table, the Warriors' logo had been hastily tacked to the wall so it would appear in the photographs and television coverage. In the far corner, a large television set had been pushed against the wall to make way for a camera tripod. It was a big room, but it was packed.

Frank was there to answer questions from the team point of view. Henshaw was there to answer any financial questions. I was there … well, you know why I was there, and Henry was there because he'd volunteered to be there.

'It's going to be tough going,' he'd said to Frank. 'The Flea is going to need a friend.' Frank had nodded.

They had rescheduled the press conference to the boardroom as soon as they had realised the number of reporters and camera crews that were going to be there. As well as all the usual sports journalists, there were people from all the newspapers up and down the country, radio stations, TV channels and two crews from Australian TV, who had flown over specially.

I felt quite important, really, for someone who had never played a game for the Warriors. I also felt really, really nervous at all the flashing bulbs and TV cameras and microphones.

I needn't have bothered. Feeling nervous that is. The questions were all for Frank, with just a few for Mr Walters about salary caps and what I was actually getting paid.

I just sat at the table next to Henry feeling like an ornament.

'What did he do to win a place in the team?' one of the Australian reporters asked, waving a spiral notepad at Frank. 'He must have impressed you with something.'

Frank looked across at me and smiled before he turned back and answered. 'You're probably expecting me to tell you about his fancy footwork and his ball-playing skills, and his speed off the mark. And all that's there. You'll see when he takes the field. Daniel is a phenomenal young player. But that wasn't what impressed me the most. What swung it for Daniel was his commitment and motivation. The very first day I met him I thought he was a brave kid for even walking into my office. During his trial he lost the ball, and most kids would have given up. But Daniel didn't. He refused to give up even when it all seemed lost, and that's the kind of attitude I need around here.'

'Patrick King, *Sports Herald*,' said a cheerful, chubby-faced man. 'Aren't you worried that Danny is going to get hurt, playing on a field with professional, adult league players? Especially teams like the Machetes.'

A low murmur ran around the room. First game of the season and the Machetes already had a reputation for tough and dirty tactics.

Henry jumped in ahead of Frank. 'I'd like to answer that question,' he said. 'And first of all it's Daniel, not Danny, but we all call him the Flea.'

Pens scribbled furiously at that.

'During training, Frank asked me to have a run at the Flea. I think his words were "squash him".'

There was laughter at that, although Frank looked quite uncomfortable. Henry continued, 'I was a bit reluctant, because I'm not a little fella,' more laughter, 'and I didn't want to hurt him. But the Flea here told me to give it my best shot. He told me, and these were his own words …' Henry paused and stood up. The TV cameras had to tilt back to keep him in the shot. He reached down and plucked me out of my seat and lifted me up on to the table, so that I was almost eye-to-eye with him. 'He told me not to chicken out.'

We faced off at each other for a moment in mock seriousness, like two heavyweight boxers weighing-in before a title fight. The room erupted in laughter and cameras flashed in a sheet of lightning.

Finally, someone asked me a question. It was a well-known sports reporter from Australian TV, Laura Grace. For some reason she spoke slowly and loudly, as if I was deaf, or stupid, or a three-year-old.

'Daniel, are you excited to be playing with the Warriors?'

What kind of a dumb question was that? I resisted the temptation to give a smart answer that would have made me seem like a brat. I also resisted the temptation to answer her in the same silly kind of voice that she asked the question. I simply said, 'Yes, it's a great honour to be on the field with players who have been my heroes for many years.'

There were lots of other questions after that, but most of them were directed at Frank, so I just smiled and nodded a lot.

ELEVEN

QUADRUPLE SCOOPLES

Henry swung by the next day. We shot around to Jason's house but he was over at Tupai's, so we drove over there. It was really cool driving around in Henry's car instead of biking everywhere all the time. They were playing stuntmen in the front yard, riding their bikes down the path, then pretending they'd just been shot by an unseen sniper and falling off, diving in a real dramatic way to the ground and rolling over and over.

Jason told me once that he had this secret hope that some big-time movie producer would be driving past just as they were doing it and would be needing some stunt-kids for a new movie they were making.

I didn't think that was very likely, but it was a fun game anyway, and I used to play it with them sometimes. Before I was a Warrior that is.

'Hey, guys,' I called.

Jason said, 'Hey, Daniel, hey, Henry.'

'Hi, chaps,' Henry replied.

Tupai looked nervous. I think he was a little awestruck by Henry. Strange, for the strongest kid in school and possibly the world.

'You coming to the game?' Jason asked.

'What game?' I asked.

'The Nuggets.' Jason looked disappointed. I felt like an idiot. I had completely forgotten that the Glenfield Giants were playing the Northcote Nuggets that afternoon. The Nuggets were much higher up the competition ladder and, being a neighbouring club, it was always a big match.

'You coming?' asked Tupai.

I looked up at Henry. 'Sorry, guys. Love to. But we've got training. You know.'

'Yeah, yeah,' Jason said, 'we know.'

Henry said, 'If you see that Phil Domane guy, can you tell him I'm sorry about calling him the boy without a brain.'

Jason laughed. I said, 'He doesn't need an apology. He's just a dork.'

'I'm sure he doesn't mean to be nasty,' Henry said. 'Most people are really good when you get to know them.'

'I don't think so,' I said. 'Phil's just plain mean.'

Henry shook his head doubtfully. Then he smiled. 'Hey, I've got a softball bat in the boot of my car. Do you guys want to play some Ball and Bat?'

'Ball and Bat?' Both Jason and Tupai looked mystified.

'You must know it. One guy pitches, another one hits, the rest field. After you hit the ball you lay the bat on the ground and whoever gets the ball tries to hit the bat with it.'

'That's Bat-Down!' Jason said. 'Yeah, sure.'

Tupai was keen too, although he still didn't say very much around Henry. We all piled into Henry's car and shot on down to Manuka Park. When we got there, Jason looked over at the entrance to the Lost Park and raised an eyebrow at me. I shook my head. The Lost Park was our secret. Not even my new friend Henry was allowed to know about that.

For a big guy Henry was really quick at Bat-Down (or Ball and Bat if you called it that). He was really co-ordinated with his pitching and catching, and if the ball went anywhere near him he'd get a hand to it for sure.

His batting was a bit of a problem for us smaller guys. The first time he hit the ball he knocked it clear out of the park. It landed somewhere down in the car park by the boat ramp.

After that, Jason had the idea of wrapping a sweatshirt around the bat whenever Henry was batting. He couldn't hit it anywhere near as far like that, so it kind of evened up the odds a little.

'Have you seen Jenny around at all?' I asked Jason. He was batting, I was backstop. He wasn't very good at it but he tried hard, and nobody minded.

'Yeah, she's around,' Jason said cautiously.

'I haven't seen her for weeks. Training and all.'

Jason swung at the ball and missed. I caught it.

'Strike one!' Henry called out.

Jason nodded. 'She watched your game. She told me.'

'Shame I didn't get on the field, eh?' I said quietly. Jason swung and missed again.

'Strike two!' Henry called.

'Yeah, shame. And I think Jenny was a bit disappointed that you forgot her birthday.'

I slapped a hand to my forehead. Jenny's birthday! I had been so tied up with training that I had completely forgotten it.

Jason swung wildly at Henry's last pitch. It was a good pitch but Jason was miles away from the ball.

'Strike three, you're out.'

I tossed the ball to Tupai, who was next-up pitcher, still shaking my head at my own stupidity. I had promised Jenny I wouldn't forget her. But I had. I made a mental note to go and see her as soon as I had a free moment.

Jason handed me the bat, laughed and ran off to the outfield. He was like that. He wasn't all that good at Bat-Down but he enjoyed himself anyway.

We just bashed around like that for the rest of the morning until lunchtime when Tupai and Jason had to go home to get ready for their game. It was great. We laughed a lot.

On the way to training Henry and I stopped for ice-creams. I asked for a double scoop. Henry ordered a quadruple scoop. He called it a quadruple scoople, but the owner of the dairy seemed to know exactly what he meant. It was an ordinary ice-cream cone but with four, count 'em, four balls of ice-cream, all different flavours, piled one on top of the other. The dairy guy had to push a milkshake straw down the middle to stop them all from falling off!

Henry smiled at me on the way out of the dairy and said, 'Don't tell Susan.'

Susan Parkes was our dietician and nutritionalist. I'm sure she would have frowned on a quadruple scoople.

The next morning I came down for breakfast before school. Dad was still there, which was unusual because he normally went off to the gallery before I woke up. He had the newspaper in front of him and he turned it around without a word.

The story hadn't just made the sports' section, it had made the front page. Almost a quarter of the page was taken up with a huge photo of me and Henry squaring off at the press conference. The headline ran: *Henry and the Flea*.

I think it was the first time Dad had really realised that what I was doing was something pretty special.

'Sit down, Danny,' he said. 'Have some breakfast.'

'Shouldn't you be at work?' I felt a little uncomfortable. I wasn't used to Dad being there in the morning, let alone wanting to talk when I had just woken up.

'I've shut the gallery for the day.' I couldn't believe it. Dad never did that! He continued, 'I didn't realise ... I guess I just didn't realise.'

'It's just another team, Dad. It's nothing.'

Dad looked at me, and I had the horrible feeling that he was going to cry, but I didn't understand why. 'No, it's not, Danny. It's not nothing. I've just been too ... I haven't been ...'

He shut his eyes for a moment. I was starting to understand what the problem was.

'Tell me about the Warriors, son.'

I didn't go to school that day.

TWELVE

DISASTER!

Dad put the art gallery up for sale the next day. I think the shock of seeing me on the front page must have had a deeper impact on him than I could have guessed. One of the Auckland Art Galleries – a really big one in the central city – was looking for a new director. Dad had already turned them down twice. I don't know why, because it was a really important job. Anyway he rang them and accepted. He didn't say a lot about it, just that he had finally come to realise what was really important in life. Much later he started calling this time the 'lost years'.

Dad came to my next game. I was so excited to see him there that I couldn't sit still on the reserves' bench. I couldn't wait to show him my skills. But I didn't play. I just sat on the bench the entire game.

Dad came to my next game too, but I didn't play in that either. The game after that was an away game, which meant flying to Australia, to Sydney in fact. Dad couldn't make it to that game. We won, but the team did it without me. I just sat on the bench.

We played in sunshine, and I sat on the bench. We played in rain, and I sat on the bench. We played in Canberra and Melbourne and even flew all the way to Townsville to play the Cowboys, and I sat on the bench. We won games we were expected to lose, we lost games we were expected to win, we drew one game against the Broncos with a last minute field goal. And all the time I sat on the bench.

Maybe I was a Warrior. Maybe I wasn't. I had stopped being sure. The season went through its usual highs and lows and all the time I sat there, taking up a space on the reserves' bench, and never getting on the field.

I tried talking to Frank about it, and Henry tried too. But all Frank would say was, 'I make decisions during the game about which reserves to bring on. You'll get your call when the time and the game is right.'

You couldn't argue with that.

One thing I was so proud of, though, was my dad. He kept on coming, to all my home games. Mum came too, to quite a few, although I know she felt quite out of place amongst all the yahooing rugby league fans. Time and time again I could count on Dad watching from the stands, even though I never took the field in front of him.

Jason came to a few games at the start of the season, but I don't think he made it after that. I really didn't have much of a chance to talk to him during the season. I hadn't seen Jenny for weeks either. Just hadn't had the time.

We won more games than we lost. We gave a couple of the better-rated sides a real hiding and other games were absolute nail-biters. And so the season finally wound to a close and we were sitting right up there in fifth place on the points table.

The top eight teams go through to the semifinals, so we were assured of a place, but the top four teams get a second life in the semis, so we were desperate to win our last match. It just happened to be against the thugs of the tournament, the Blacktown Machetes.

The Machetes had bullied and bumped their way into second place on the table, right behind the Brisbane Broncos, who had had an incredible season, losing only one game. It didn't really matter to the Machetes whether they won or lost this last game, but it was vitally important to us. Somehow, though, all of us knew that they were going to be playing for keeps, no matter what the stakes were.

I took my usual seat on the reserves' bench, next to George, who was usually a run-on player but was still getting over a hamstring injury.

The first half was scoreless, just a lot of crash and bash as we had come to expect against the Machetes. Frank's face was grim at half-time. Falofa, Nicholson and Kris had all come off and were not going back on the field that day. We didn't know it then, but Nicholson would not get back on the field that year, thanks to a nasty bone fracture in his knee.

The changing room is a surprisingly cold place. No matter how high you turn up the heating it always feels cold. Something to do with the concrete walls and its location in the bowels of the grandstand. It's a bit of a dungeon really. At half-time, when the coach isn't happy, it can seem even colder.

'They're hammering us,' Frank said in a voice full of fury. 'It's not pretty and it's not legal but they're getting away with it. We can't avoid it and there's only one thing to do.' He looked around at us all. 'You've got to hammer back. Don't let them get away with it. Stand up for yourselves. But don't do anything illegal.'

We all knew what he meant. He meant 'give them as good as they gave.' And 'don't do anything illegal' simply meant 'don't get caught'.

'You've got to show them you're not scared of them or they are going to eat you alive.'

I saw Henry shake his head, just slightly. He wasn't going to argue with the coach, especially not in the middle of a crucial match, but he wasn't the sort to play dirty, no matter what was going on with the other team. You had to respect him for that.

The second half started the same way the first had, bash, crash and smash, only this time it wasn't just our guys who got up rubbing their heads or their arms after a hard tackle. There was another difference too, and that difference was Henry.

Henry, it seemed, had decided to win the match, regardless of how the other team was playing. He went at the line like a demolition ball, knocking players out of the way, charging over the top of others. Every time he touched the ball he made a ten to twenty metre gain. It was fantastic rugby league.

It was only a matter of time before one of his buffeting runs opened up a gap in their defences and let Ainsley scoot through for a try. The deadlock was broken. Then the miracle happened.

Henry had played over a hundred first class games for the Warriors and never scored a try. To be honest, front rowers don't score tries all that often, that's left to the backs and the wingers after the front rowers have done their argy-bargy stuff.

This time, though, Henry crashed through a couple of defenders and flipped the ball out to Bazza, who carved a line up through the middle of the Machetes until Rumble Bean brought him crashing down hard, close to the line.

He was up quick though, and Henry, who was closest, played hooker. That's not usually the job of a front row forward either! Bazza toed the ball back and Henry picked it up like a piece of fruit. He dummied a pass to Ricky, who had closed in and was running a tight angle towards the line. Then Henry just hurled himself at the Machetes' defence. He exploded through three of them and dropped over the line for a try.

I was jumping up and down on the bench seat, shouting at the top of my lungs. Henry stood up and looked over to me and saluted like a sergeant major. I stood ramrod straight and saluted back and we both laughed. The Machetes huddled behind their line while Ainsley kicked the conversion and I noticed Rumble Bean casting a couple of evil glances at Henry.

I shivered, even though it was quite a warm day.

Three sets of six later, Rumble struck like a venomous snake. They were clever how they planned it, and clever how they did it, but that didn't make it any less mean.

Henry had the ball; he had bounced off Alistair, one of their forwards, and was tussling with a couple more Machetes, still making progress towards the try line. That was when I noticed that the two Machetes didn't really seem to be trying to tackle him. They were just sort of holding him, pulling one of his arms away from his body. A sharp movement caught my eye. Rumble Bean was arrowing in like a guided missile, knees pumping, shoulder dropped. The other two weren't tackling Henry, they were turning him into a target.

'Henry!' I shouted from the other side of the field, but he could never have heard me and it was far too late anyway. 'Henry!'

Rumble smashed into Henry's outstretched arm with a crack that I could hear and feel right across the park. Henry spun around and toppled over, Bean's knee crashing into the side of his head as he fell. The ball came out as he hit the ground.

Rumble was on the loose ball in a second and I didn't even see him dive over our line for the try. I was still watching Henry, who hadn't moved since he had crashed to the ground.

A moment later the stretcher buggy was called and it took six guys to lift Henry on to the back of the machine. Six players. They wouldn't let the trainers do it, just pushed them out of the way and lifted the stretcher themselves. They all stood in a line as a gesture of respect as the buggy drove off towards the sideline. My heart felt like it had stopped. It took me a long time to realise that old Andy the trainer was talking to me.

'What?' I said vacantly. 'I don't understand.'

Andy waved his hand at the reserves' bench and suddenly I did understand. I was the last reserve. So many of our guys had been taken off the park with injuries that I was the only one left to fill out the squad.

'Henry, I've gotta go see Henry,' I stammered. 'He's been hurt.'

Andy said nothing and just passed me the radio.

'Frank, it's Flea. I can't …'

'Yes, you can,' Frank cut me off. 'We'll look after Henry. You get on the field and show me that it's not all just talk and fancy moves in training.'

I had no choice then, and, with Henry weighing heavily on my mind, I stripped off my tracksuit and jogged slowly on to the pitch.

I played the last fifteen minutes of that match, and for thirteen of them the ball came nowhere near me. The rest of the team played as if I wasn't on the park. They didn't pass me the ball and they slid across in front of me whenever an attack was looming. They were playing like a twelve man squad against thirteen and so it was no surprise that the Machetes ran in two quick tries. They missed both conversions though, which left the score at fourteen to twelve with two minutes to go.

If you're on a rugby field that long though, sooner or later the ball has to come your way, and eventually it did, in the hands of the man himself, Rumble Bean, who had picked it up from broken play and found himself in the open with just me between him and the match-winning try.

It was all too easy really. I held my ground in front of him the way I had with Henry in training. He stuck out an arm in a vicious fend but I sidestepped and ankle-tapped him, just like before. I toed the ball out, picked it up and weaved a fiery path right through the centre of the Machetes' pack before sliding over for my first-ever professional rugby league try.

Henry and I had both scored our first tries in the same match! I hoped like anything that he was OK. I looked up and noticed Rumble Bean staring at me. Not staring really, more like giving me the evil eye. I did my best Crazy Jason glare right back at him.

Ainsley converted and a moment or so later the final whistle sounded. We had won, but it didn't feel like a victory to me. There had been no word from the hospital and the whole team was holding its breath waiting to hear about Henry.

Frank eventually brought the news into the changing room while we were cleaning up after the game.

'We've heard from the hospital,' he said quietly and the room went instantly silent. 'He has concussion and a dislocated shoulder. They're X-raying to see if anything is broken. We'll know in a few days if we'll have him back for the semifinals.'

I was surrounded by players I had come to know well, and many of them I called my friends. But never in my life have I felt so dreadfully alone.

We flew back from Australia on Sunday morning and I biked straight over to Jason's place to see if he had watched the match. Seen me play. Seen me score. His mum said he was down at the park with the boys, so I headed down there.

Their bikes were at the boat ramp but Manuka Park was empty, so I knew they'd be in the Lost Park.

I burst down the secret track and out into the Lost Park yahooing like a scatterbrain. But then I stopped. I stopped and I shut up. Because things weren't right. Things were very wrong.

Jenny was there, for a start. She might have been my girlfriend but she was still a girl, and we'd vowed never to tell any girls about the Lost Park.

Jason and Tupai were running around the fort, playing pirates or something like that, and Fizzer was up in the Spitfire.

But there was someone else. Someone sitting with Jenny on the tractor, with his arm around her shoulders. It seemed that Jenny had got herself a new boyfriend.

That hurt. I knew it was my own fault for being away all the time, for missing her birthday, but it still hurt. They all looked around when I came bursting through the track. Then Jenny moved her head, and I saw who she was sitting with.

It was the boy without a brain. Phil Domane.

THIRTEEN

THE SMART FART

Looking back, I know I felt hurt about Jenny and Phil, but that was nothing compared to how wounded I felt that Phil had been invited to the Lost Park. The Lost Park was private. It was ours. Me and Jason and Fizzer and Tupai. Except that now it seemed to be Phil and Jason and Fizzer and Tupai.

Jenny kind of covered her face and looked at the ground. Jason climbed down from the fort and walked over. He stood awkwardly in front of me and didn't say anything at first.

'Hi, Daniel,' he said eventually. 'Or is it Flea now?'

'Still Daniel,' I said calmly. 'I …'

I stopped at that, spun around on my heels and ran back into the track. I missed my footing on the rotten, old bridge and crashed into the creek, coming up covered in mud and sludgy water. Then Jason was beside me and we walked back to Manuka Park together.

'I can't believe you told Phil about the Lost Park,' I said, struggling not to cry like a little kid. 'I just can't believe it.'

'You haven't been around much,' Jason said. 'You haven't

been around at all really and Phil's not such a bad guy. He just thinks you're a bit of a smart fart, and …'

He stopped.

'And what?' I asked tightly.

'Well. Well, you are a bit of a smart fart sometimes. I mean, I don't care, but you haven't been here and …'

I blinked a couple of times and left him standing there with his mouth gaping open. I didn't even bother about my bike, I just sprinted up the road from the park and jogged all the way back home. I was hot and I was cold. Hot from the running, cold from the wet clothes. I hardly noticed though. How could they? How could Jason? Just because I'd been busy with my team. It just wasn't fair.

And, on top of all that, he'd called me a smart fart. In just one morning Jason had gone from my good friend to my sworn enemy.

By the evening I was so worked up about it that I'd made a papier mâché voodoo doll of Jason and was busy sticking pins in it. That was when the telephone rang. Dad answered it.

'It's for you, Danny … Daniel,' he called from the hall.

'I'm not here,' I called back.

'He says he's not here.' Dad was trying to be funny; it just made me more angry. Jason and the rest of those guys could go get …

'It's that Henry chap from your team.'

I dropped the voodoo doll and was by the phone before Dad had finished his sentence. I snatched away the receiver.

'Hi, Henry.'

'Hi, mate, how's it going?'

'It's … OK. How are you feeling? Are you going to be all right?'

'I'm a bit sore. They had to relocate my shoulder. No broken bones though, so I'll be back for the semis. Bad luck, eh?'

I exhaled slowly. That was a huge relief. I had been afraid Henry had been seriously injured. I thought carefully about what I said next. 'It wasn't bad luck, Henry, it was deliberate.'

'You reckon?'

'I know. I saw Rumble lining up to get you. They wanted you out of the game.'

There was a long silence from the hospital in Australia.

'That's not nice.'

Then I wished I hadn't said it. Henry was just a simple guy. He had his own view of the world. And it wasn't a view in which people like Rumble Bean would deliberately set out to break a player's arm.

Because that was what Rumble had intended to do, I had no doubt. I could see the whole thing over and over in my mind, like an action replay. The way he had crashed into Henry's arm would have snapped anyone else's like a twig. He'd still managed to do some serious damage, even to a meat-mountain like Henry. I changed the subject.

'Congratulations on your first-ever try.'

'Congratulations yourself!'

'When are you back?'

'Wednesday. They're flying me back business class, for the comfort.'

'Lucky beggar.'

We chatted a bit more, then Henry rang off. Now, there was a guy who'd be loyal to his friends, I thought, even if they were out of touch for a bit.

FOURTEEN

GROWING DOWN

If I thought my first press conference was a major event, the second made it look like a Sunday school picnic.

The first time the story was about my selection for the Warriors. This time it was about my playing a game and scoring the winning try. All the reporters were there from the previous press conference plus CNN, ESPN, BBC, in fact the whole alphabet from ABC to XYZ.

Henry wasn't there this time. That was a shame, and I know he wanted to be there to lend some moral support, but he was still in hospital.

My dad came though, and sat by my side the whole time. It was good having him there. This time the questions were sharper and directed at me. All you have to do to be taken seriously by the world's media, it seems, is to score the winning try in a professional rugby league game. If you are a thirteen-year-old boy that is.

The story made the front page again, made the top three stories on the evening news on both the main TV channels, was a human interest story on CNN and a lead on ESPN right around the world. Sky had it, the radio stations carried it, you would have thought I'd just invented a cure for cancer the way they all went on.

It didn't stop with that one game either. From that moment on, if I took the field, it made the news. Of course, it helped that I scored tries in all of our semifinal games, and that we won all the games.

The fastest Warrior of all time, they called me, a title that used to belong to Ricky Albany.

Henry missed the first game but was fully fit for the second, against the Broncos, and we played like demons, eventually taking the mighty Broncos down 34 to 28 and knocking them out of the tournament.

The other team that was knocking teams aside with a flyswatter was the Machetes. They hadn't been expected to do very well this season but when it came down to the wire it was them and us. The Machetes versus the Warriors for the season Grand Final.

We flew to Australia a week before the Final and the Sydney Roosters lent us their fields and facilities for the lead-up training. Nice of them really.

The week was full of activities. We were treated like movie stars and the official Grand Final Breakfast was something else again.

On the morning of the big day I woke up extra early. I just couldn't sleep. I sort of dreamed my way all through the team's carefully calibrated, nutritionally balanced breakfast and the rest of the day passed in a bit of a blur. Right up until just before game time.

Frank called me up into the Coaches' box as preparations for the Grand Final swirled all around us. He motioned for the others to leave and asked me to sit down. I sat, feeling like the same brave twelve-year-old with the messy black hair and freckles who had sat in front of Frank all those months ago.

'You're a Warrior, kid,' he said, 'and one of the best I've got. And you're only thirteen years old. What are you going to be like when you're twenty?'

I just smiled and shook my head. Frank was heading somewhere but, unusually for him, he was taking a roundabout way of getting there. He said, 'I strongly believe that if it wasn't for you, we wouldn't be in this Grand Final this year.'

'The first day I met you, I promised you that if you put me in the team, you'd win the premiership.'

Frank nodded, then shook his head as well. 'I remember, but we haven't won the premiership yet, we've still got to beat the Machetes one more time. And that's what I wanted to talk to you about.'

I was getting a strangely uncomfortable feeling, but I let him continue.

'You've seen the style of league the Machetes have been playing. If I put you on the field in the Grand Final I might as well paint a target on your forehead.'

This was not sounding good. 'Do you want to win the premiership?' I asked, a bit nervously.

'Yes, I do, kid. Yes I do. I want to win the premiership very much. But ask me another question. Ask me if I want to win it, if it means you get seriously injured … or worse. Then the answer is no. No, I'd give it away in a millisecond.'

'I won't get hurt. I can look after myself.'

'Flea, Daniel, you could win the game for us today. You know that, I know that, and you can bet your rugby boots that the Machetes know that. They'll target you and they'll hurt you to take you out of the game. Do you understand that? You saw what they did to that monster Henry. What is going to happen to a scrawny insect like you?'

'Scrawny!'

Frank held up a hand so I'd know not to get angry. 'You get injured today, and you might not be playing when you're twenty. You might not be walking.'

'I can handle it.'

'I don't want you to.'

'Frank …'

'Flea, listen to me. If it was entirely up to me I wouldn't even have you on the reserves' bench today. I'm not going to put you on the field, so really you're just taking up a space that I could have used for someone else. But you know what?'

'What?'

'I couldn't do that. You've become a bit of a star. If I had named the team for the Grand Final and hadn't named you in it somewhere, I'd be lynched by the fans. So you'll be on the bench. And that's where you'll stay. And don't go complaining to me, or anyone else, about it. The decision is mine and the decision is final.'

I was blinking back tears as we were waiting in the dressing room for the pre-match entertainment to finish.

Henry saw at once that something was wrong but he couldn't work out what.

'You OK, Flea?'

'Yeah, I guess.'

'What did Frank want?'

'Just a chat.'

'You are playing today, aren't you?'

I looked down the tunnel, away from my friend, and told him. 'I'll be on the bench, in my usual place.'

'That's good.' Henry looked relieved. 'I was afraid he wasn't going to play you. Have Jason or any of your friends come over for the game?'

He must have seen something in my face because he asked, 'What's going on, Flea?'

And so I told him.

I told him about Jason and Jenny, and Phil and Lost Parks and Smart Farts and everything except the voodoo doll. I was a bit embarrassed about that.

Henry just looked at me. For a very long time. He didn't say anything. Neither did I because I knew Henry well enough to know what that silence meant, and we both felt comfortable with it. Finally he said, 'I know what it's like to be thirteen.'

There was a huge cheer from the stadium for some part of the pre-match.

'When you're thirteen, you just want to be fourteen. When you're fourteen you can't wait until you're fifteen. Fifteen wants to be sixteen, and on it goes. And then you get to thirty.'

'And you want to be thirty-one?'

'No.' There was a trace of regret in Henry's voice. 'You'd give anything to be thirteen again.'

He spoke with a smile that softened the words he had to say but did not change the meaning. 'Flea, if you live to be a hundred and thirteen, you will never again have friends like those you have when you are thirteen. We're buddies. And I like being your buddy. But Jason's your mate.'

I said sullenly, 'If he was my mate he wouldn't have called me a smart fart. And he certainly wouldn't have told Phil about the Lost Park!'

'OK. Jason did a bad thing.' Henry looked me straight in the eye, the way he did when he was giving me advice about playing league. 'He did a bad thing. It doesn't make him a bad person.'

I blinked twice and Henry froze. My breath caught in my throat. I didn't often, well almost never, use the Thing when I was just talking to people, but I needed time to think.

Jason did a bad thing. It doesn't make him a bad person.

Henry wasn't very smart. He was big, strong and athletic, but he was a simple kind of guy and he was the first to admit it. Yet somehow he had a simple way of looking at things that cut through all the rubbish that the rest of us had to think about. He was right. As much as I hated to admit it, he was right.

Henry, in slow motion, was opening his mouth to speak and I flicked back into normal time. 'How many good things has Jason done?'

'Well …' I could think of hundreds, not the least of which was that time at my try-out when just his belief in me had got me into the Warriors' team. 'Lots, I guess.'

'The way I see it, when you do something good, that's like making a deposit in your bank account.'

'I don't have a bank account,' I interrupted, but continued quickly, 'but I see your point.'

Henry continued as if I hadn't spoken. 'Doing good builds up credit in the account. Doing something bad is like making a withdrawal. If you do too many bad things, well … you end up in overdraft and I guess at that stage you gotta wonder if the person is really your friend.'

I said quietly, 'I understand.'

'So is Jason in credit or overdraft at the moment?'

'He's in credit. A lot of credit.'

'So …' Henry smiled that big, simple smile of his. 'That's that then.'

We got our call and stood up to move out into the tunnel. I said, 'Thanks, Henry.'

'That's what buddies are for. Have a blinder today.'

'You too, mate. You too.'

Looking back now, that's the moment I can pick when I started to 'grow down'. I'd been trying so hard to grow up quickly that I had missed out on a lot of what being a kid was all about. So I grew down. I just sort of settled into being a kid again.

FIFTEEN

THE GRAND FINAL

The Grand Final started well. In fact the first half was another tight, tense game of rugby league between two evenly matched sides. Which was all very well, but the second half was a nightmare.

The Grand Final was at the massive Stadium Australia that had been built for the Sydney Olympics. The atmosphere at a Final is like no other game, from the pre-game entertainment on.

The Machetes ran out first but we had a surprise in store for the crowd. Rather than run out from the tunnel in the traditional way, we waited for our music. It had all been arranged in advance. It was *Whiney Whiney* by Willi One Blood; the song Henry had played to me in the car. It was my idea, but the whole team had got behind it, and even Frank thought it was great.

We didn't run out, instead we all formed a single file and slow-marched out in this kind of Egyptian style. The crowd roared. They loved it! The Machetes just stood around on the pitch shaking their heads. They had been totally upstaged, and they knew it.

You can play all the club rugby league you like, you can play sell-out games at your home stadium and sit in front of TV cameras broadcasting your picture to millions of people around the world, but until you've stood on the pitch in front of the solid wall of sound of eighty thousand roaring rugby league fans at an NRL Grand Final you can't imagine what it feels like. Everything that had gone before suddenly seemed dull and grey compared to the colour and spectacle of the Grand Final.

They played the national anthems of New Zealand and Australia before the match. I don't know why because it wasn't actually an international, but it was still stirring.

I sat back on my seat on the reserves' bench after the anthem and prayed that Frank would let me play. He didn't, of course, and I caught Ricky Albany, the second-fastest Warrior of all time, smirking at me just before kick-off, which soured things a bit.

The first half was a thrilling tug of war. It took twenty minutes for a single point to go on the board, and that was a penalty to the Machetes. Five minutes later, though, Ricky touched down in the corner and Fuller converted the try to make the score six: two.

The Machetes hit back just before half-time and missed the conversion, so the score came to six all. All that effort and both teams were in exactly the same position as when they had started the match.

The second half was just embarrassing. Ainsley, who has the safest hands in the competition, fumbled the ball on the kick-off and the Machetes scored from the scrum that followed. We looked like we might hit back a few moments later, but Streakson, their flying winger, intercepted Bazza's pass to Brownie and ran eighty metres to score another try. By the time Rumble Bean had barged over for a third unanswered try in the seventy-sixth minute it was looking like a rout. Rene Philips converted the try and from that moment on the game was lost.

We were sixteen points down with just over three minutes to go. To win we would have to score three tries, and convert them. It just wasn't possible. The commentators were already talking about a great Machetes' victory and how it had capped off a stellar first year for the club, whatever that means.

Frank had gone quiet. Terrifyingly quiet. The walkie-talkies in the trainers' hands were empty of his normal crackly chatter. I guess on his mind must have been the missed tackles, the bungled try and the ref's decisions, which had gone against us all night. This time I think he had really thought we could win it. A first for the club. A first in the history of the competition. Now just a might-have-been.

A Mexican wave was running around the ground, congratulating the Machetes. It passed behind me with a roar and a couple of empty paper cups and bits of paper floated down to the ground in front of me.

I turned to old Andy, sitting beside me on the reserves'

bench, resting his legs. 'Give me your radio.' He passed it over with an expression that said, 'Too late, why bother?'

'Frank,' I said urgently, 'it's Flea.'

Nearly ten seconds of the game ticked over while I waited for him to reply, and there just weren't that many seconds left in the game.

'Yes, Flea?'

'Put me on. Please, boss.'

'It's over, Flea. The game is over.' His voice sounded tired.

'I know, boss. So do the Machetes. So they're not likely to have a go at me, are they? There're three minutes left. Put me on, just so I can tell my kids one day that I ran on to the field in a Grand Final.' Another vital five seconds went by.

'All right. It can't do any harm. Get yourself ready. And don't get yourself hurt.'

Twenty seconds later I was on the field. In the Grand Final. In front of eighty thousand people.

Fuller was getting ready to kick-off, but he noticed me and took his time, tipping me a wink as I ran into position. I tapped my chest and pointed to the far corner of the field. He shook his head. I gave him my best Crazy Jason glare and tapped my chest again twice. He glanced at Henry, who had seen me and was nodding his head at Fuller. Fuller shrugged and lined up for the kick.

I gave him the eagle sign, meaning 'give it wings'. Kick it as far as you can.

He launched himself at the ball and gave it a whack it'll never forget. The moment he started to run, I blinked into the Thing and was over the line in the same second that his boot hit the leather. The ball really did soar and, for a brief moment, I was afraid it was going to go dead on the fall, but it started to drop, just a couple of metres in from the Machetes' goal line. Floridiana lined himself up to catch it. Like a true league professional his eyes never left the ball. Nor did he have any reason to take his eyes off it. There was no way any of the Warriors were going to get from the halfway mark down to the Machetes' goal line in time to contest the ball.

Except for me of course.

The ball floated gently down into his arms, but, just before it got there, I leaped into the air, caught the ball, trotted the couple of remaining metres to the goal line and cruised around the back behind the posts to make it easier for the conversion.

Floridiana was still waiting there for the ball long after I had scored the try! Ainsley converted with ease and we were only ten points behind. With one minute and fifty seconds left on the clock.

The second try was even easier. Longer, easier, and a lot more dangerous. Brownie came up to me while the Machetes were setting up for kick-off.

'Flea,' he said with a voice full of concern. 'Watch yourself. I overheard a couple of the Machetes. They're talking about a Flea sandwich.' Brownie trotted back into position, leaving me nervous and a little bit shocked.

The commentators called it a gang-tackle. Henry called it a sandwich. It wasn't quite illegal, as long as it wasn't late, or high, but it was definitely nasty. Two or three of the opposition try to hit you at the same time from different directions. They don't care about making the tackle, just about hitting you as hard as they can. If you're the unlucky player, you become the meat in a very hard sandwich. If you're lucky, you'll just get winded. If you're lucky!

The Machetes kicked off, another good, long kick, although they did have the wind behind them to make it easier. The ball actually crossed our goal line and Fuller took it in the in-goal area. He skipped forward a couple of paces and passed it out to Henry, expecting Henry to start one of his long bullocking runs.

Except Henry didn't. He looked at me and I nodded. So Henry gave me the ball. I darted forward at the Machetes' line. If it hadn't been for the Thing I probably would never have seen the sandwich coming, and even so it was lucky that Brownie had warned me.

Nick and Alistair, two of the biggest, ugliest Machetes forwards were closing in. One from the left, one from the right. Their hands were down, a sure sign of a shoulder charge. And the two of them meant that Brownie was right. It was a shoulder sandwich.

When you're thirteen, running in the Grand Final, with the Thing to help you, you are full of confidence. At least I was. And, although I saw the sandwich coming, I was sure I could deal with it. So I didn't change my course at all. I just ran straight into the looming trap.

Nick and Alistair were big and strong, but they were also fast. Nick was flying in from the left and Alistair was hurtling in from the right. They were zeroing in on to a target and that target was me. Five metres away, then four, three, two, one and I stopped dead in my tracks. It was one of my favourite tricks.

I stopped dead and Nick and Alistair crashed into where I would rightly have been if I had kept going. Except I wasn't there, so they just crashed into each other. It was like a train wreck with arms and legs flailing everywhere, and the thud of the bodies colliding was so loud that I felt it like a thud on my chest. Then they bounced off each other leaving a lovely little hole in the defensive line, which I skipped through with a wonderful feeling of joy and adrenalin.

That left just Rumble Bean to beat, and he was easy. I ran to the left then stepped off my left foot and changed direction abruptly to the right. Bean was expecting that, though, and stepped off his own foot, changing direction with me. But I had been expecting that too, and my left foot step was only a feint. I kept going to the left, and Bean was totally wrong-footed. He had one leg going one way and the other leg going the other way and his hand went down on the ground behind him. He looked exactly like he was playing a game of twister with himself!

Give him credit though. He was up in a flash and chasing hard. I didn't run too fast. I wanted to keep it interesting for the punters, and I suppose a part of me wanted to show off and annoy Bean a little. So I kept just ahead of him, just out of range of his arms, or a diving ankle-tap. And like that the two of us ran down to the Machetes' goal line.

I ducked right under the centre of the sticks and dotted the ball down, then jogged a few steps along the in-goal area, wagging my finger at the crowd as if they had been naughty. They erupted out of their seats, even though most of them were Machetes' fans. But there was one face that wasn't. A Machetes' fan that is. I looked up into the crowd, into a sea of eighty thousand faces, and somehow I looked straight into the eyes of Jason Kirk.

He was sitting next to his dad; they must have flown over for the Final. He waved and I gave him a huge grin, and that's when Bean hit me from behind in a late tackle. It was late, it was hard, and it was deliberate. And I wasn't expecting it because you're not allowed to tackle someone after they have scored a try. It's in the rule book!

I felt like I had been hit in the back with a tree. All the wind was knocked out of me and my head hit the turf, hard. Somehow I managed to sit up, but the entire grandstand was swimming in a huge circle around my head. I tried to stand but just fell over and from where I fell I could see the grandstand clock. Sixty seconds to go. Then Henry's huge arm was around my shoulders and he half carried me back to our end of the field while Ainsley slotted the ball between the posts for the conversion. We were four points behind.

SIXTEEN

SIXTY SECONDS

Two tries in two minutes. One minute to play and we were just four points behind. The maths was simple. If we could score another try we'd equalise. If we could convert that try we'd win. I shook my head, trying to clear it. I still don't know why Bean hadn't been sent off, or at least penalised, for that late tackle on me. You can't tackle a player after he's scored a try! The trainers were all around me, checking that I was OK. I wasn't, but I couldn't let them know that.

The Machetes lined up for kick-off, and it was pretty obvious that they were going to try a short kick-off and try and get the ball back themselves. If they did then they could probably soak up the last sixty seconds of the game with some slow play-of-the-balls and put it out on the last tackle to eat up more time.

I blinked twice as I did the Thing, to get ready for the kick. But nothing happened. Maybe I was still woozy from the tackle. Maybe the Thing was broken? I didn't know what caused the Thing to happen, so I had no idea what might cause it to stop happening. But, for whatever reason, the

Thing would not happen. I tried again, and again, and slowly it dawned on me that I was out on a rugby field, in the middle of a Grand Final, with twenty-five hard, professional rugby players, most of them twice my age. And the Thing that had got me there was not working.

My legs felt weak and for the first time I felt butterflies in my tummy. Except I don't think these were butterflies, they felt more like small birds.

I turned to Henry as Carver lined up the kick-off for the Machetes. 'Henry,' I called urgently, 'I can't do this!'

Henry looked carefully at me. As always he didn't doubt, argue or ask questions. He just instinctively knew something was wrong.

'Look around, Flea. There's eighty thousand people here who think you can. So whether you can or not, you've got to try your best. For all of them. For your fans.'

The sound of a boot on leather interrupted him. Carver had kicked off. He had kicked, not towards my wing, but towards Ricky Albany's. No doubt they wanted to keep the ball as far away from me as possible. If only they knew! I tried the Thing again, but it was still broken.

Henry called to me out of the corner of his mouth, without taking his eyes off play. 'Get me the ball, then get behind me. I'll make you a hole the size of Cook Strait in their line, all you gotta do is run through it.'

Yeah, right, I thought, Henry always sees things so simply. He'll just make a hole and I'll run through it, without the Thing!

The ball came rocketing down out of the air just over the ten metre mark. Any less and it would have been a penalty. Michaels went high for our side but suddenly there were blue jumpers everywhere as the Machetes rushed up to try and reclaim the kick. Rumble Bean took out Michaels with a shoulder, knocking him backwards in the air, totally illegal of course, but in that whirling storm of blue and black bodies it was hard to see what was going on. Then there was just this sea of blue and the Machetes' hands stretched up to grab the ball. We were lost for sure.

But somehow, out of nowhere, up through the middle of the hurricane came a flying, black jumper and Ricky Road Runner Albany, the second-fastest Warrior of all time, flew through the air like Michael Jordan, gathered the ball as it dropped towards the clutching hands of the Machetes, and crashed through the players to the ground.

Alastair and Nick, the two Machetes forwards, grabbed at him and smothered him in a tackle, but we had the ball!

Ricky played the ball and Ainsley rushed in at hooker, passing the ball to Bazza, who got smashed by a gang tackle. He was up quick though and played the ball, although he dropped to his knees afterwards and put his head down for a moment.

Ainsley played hooker again and doubled around with Brownie, who charged straight at the line and nearly got a pass away before one of the Machetes clamped a hand around his arm.

Brownie played the ball, Des played hooker and passed it back infield to Ainsley, who chip-kicked it over the top of

Rumble Bean's head and darted around him to regather the ball. Or he would have, except Rumble tripped him and Ainsley went sprawling. Streakson, the Machetes' pacy winger, pulled in the ball and shot at the gap where Ainsley had been. He left-footed Brownie and was away down the field with just our full-back to beat, when the whistle went. Hanson, the referee, had seen the trip.

Most of our team were applauding as Streakson, with a scowl a mile wide, brought the ball back to the spot that Hanson marked with his heel.

There was no question of kicking for a penalty goal, that would have gained us just two points, not enough to win, and no time left for another try.

So Ainsley kicked for the sideline, which took us to just twenty metres from the Machetes' goal line.

The two teams lined up at each other, seconds ticking away. I prayed the ball would stay on the far side of the field. Then Brownie tapped the ball with his foot and, as Jason would say, it all went as wild as thunder in a bucket.

Brownie tapped and passed to Ainsley who batted it along to Bazza. It was what they call a hospital pass. Bazza was about to get monstered by Chugs and Mouldren. You gotta admire Bazza though, he knew what to do. He turned his back on the tacklers to protect the ball and shot it out the back to Pacman, who flung it backwards to George. Suddenly we were thirty metres away from the goal line. We'd gone back ten metres and just then the siren sounded for the end of the game.

The game wasn't over though. It wasn't over until the ref blew his whistle, and he couldn't do that until the ball went to ground, or was put dead.

George ran up five metres and passed to his right. And that's how the ball got to Henry. What happened next was not a lot short of a miracle.

Henry did exactly what he had said he was going to do. He tucked the ball under that huge left arm, let out a roar that sounded like Tyrannosaurus Rex with a really bad headache and let rip at the line.

Rene Phillips had the bad luck to be first in his line of fire. He got batted aside like a moth. Clancy and Carver hit Henry hard, Clancy around the legs and Carver about the waist. It slowed him a little but didn't look even slightly like stopping him. He was a bull, no, more like a bulldozer. Clancy hung on to Henry's ankle desperately, all the while trying to latch on to the other ankle and pull him down.

Ackland went flying in from the side and smashed the ball-carrying arm, trying to jolt the ball loose. He might just as well have tried to hammer in a nail with a feather. Ackland clung on though. Henry didn't seem to care. He crossed the twenty metre mark like a runaway concrete truck, and that's when Banter leaped on the top and Floridiana hit him from the right.

Nobody has ever seen anything like it, before or since. Henry was carrying what seemed like half the Machetes team, and dragging another along the ground. And he was still going!

Two more Machetes closed in from the left, and Froder and the winger raced in from the right. Rumble Bean stood his ground in front of the whole shebang, waiting for the juggernaut to reach him.

Right then, though, Clancy managed to get his arms around Henry's other tree-stump of a leg and he hugged Henry's ankles for dear life.

It doesn't matter how big you are, it doesn't matter how strong you are. If your ankles are tied together you cannot run.

The juggernaut stopped. It waited for a moment, then slowly, with another roar like the dying scream of a dinosaur, the mass of bodies began to topple forwards.

Somehow, in the midst of all that highly paid, rugby league flesh and bone, a burly arm poked out, holding the ball, and tossed it backwards to me.

Henry couldn't have seen me. He had no way of knowing where I'd be. And yet, without looking, he tossed the ball straight into my arms. The commentators called it a wild pass, a speculator, tossed in the hope that someone would be there. They were wrong though. Henry may not have been able to see me, but he knew *exactly* where I'd be.

The ball came backwards as if in slow motion, but it wasn't really slow motion because the Thing was still broken. I grabbed it and clutched it to my chest.

To the left I had two Machetes; to the right I had two more. In front of me was a tangled mass, a mountain of blue jumpers with Henry at the bottom of it all. Behind that was the sneering face of Dell (Rumble) Bean.

There was no way to go, there was no time to think. So I didn't think. I just ran. Somewhere in the back of my head were some words that Frank had once said to me, a hundred years ago. *Don't do what the opposition expects you to do.* I didn't. I ran straight at the mountain in front of me. I wasn't even sure if that was legal.

I trod on Clancy's leg, skipped up Carver's back, jumped on to another bit of someone, Floridiana I think, and leaped off the top of the huge pile of bodies, right at Rumble Bean.

He certainly wasn't expecting it. No one would have been. It's not often that you get players coming at you through the air at head height. He grabbed up at me but he was too slow. Way too slow.

My foot landed on his shoulder and, before he could do anything, I used him as a springboard, launching myself into space, just five metres from the Machetes' line.

I dived over the line and somehow landed on my feet. The crowd was on theirs too. The only thing was, the impact of the landing, from that height, was a jarring jolt. The ball came loose even as my legs buckled underneath me and I crashed to the ground.

The ball spun up in the air, lazily turning end to end. It began to drop, arrowing down just in front of me. I stretched out and grabbed it, an inch above the turf. The crowd was just about exploding. I planted the ball on the grass and we were suddenly four points richer. The whistle blew for the try.

Two strong hands lifted me off the deck and hoisted me into the air like a trophy. I looked down at the smiling face of Ricky Albany.

'You're OK, Flea,' he said. 'You're OK.' At least I think that's what he said, but it was hard to hear above all the screaming fans and shouts from my team-mates. Ricky lifted me up on to Henry's broad shoulders. That's when I noticed Henry was bleeding from a cut above his eye. It didn't seem to bother him though.

After all that, the conversion was a bit of an anticlimax. Ainsley slotted it over without even trying, or so it seemed. The game was ours and we were surrounded, the other players just wanting to hug us or pat us on the back.

Not just our own players either, a lot of the Machetes' players seemed just as excited, even though they'd lost the Grand Final. It takes a big player to genuinely congratulate the winning team when you've just lost the biggest match of your life, and I learned a lot of respect for some of those Machetes after that.

Not Rumble Bean though. He slunk off and didn't even shake anyone's hand. He didn't last long with the team after that either. Last I heard he was playing in some cold, dank place somewhere in England.

Henry carried me off the field with the rest of the team mobbing all around him and the crowd still screaming with excitement.

And that was the last game of professional rugby league I ever played.

SEVENTEEN

GOOD FRIENDS

The celebrations lasted for days. So did the interest from the world's media. There were endless interviews and press conferences and photo sessions. It was all a bit much really. Through it all, though, Henry was right there by my side, looking out for me. So was my dad and I felt really good about that. When things were getting a bit tough or I was getting a bit overwhelmed they would step in, or get me out of there if needs be. Nobody was going to argue with Henry Knight!

So it was nearly a week before I got back to Glenfield and caught up with Jason. Henry drove me around to Jason's house but Jason wasn't there, so I suggested we try the Lost Park.

'Worth a try,' big Henry said. 'And anyway I'm dying to see this place.'

'You're not allowed to tell anyone about it!' I warned. 'Or I'll beat you up.'

Henry's head just about touched the roof of the car and

he looked down at me from that height and laughed. 'I promise.'

We saw Jason cycling back from the park and I wound down my window and called to him to turn around and meet us down there.

We waited for him by the secret path and the three of us walked through the track together. Henry had to jump across the creek 'cos he didn't think the old, rotten bridge would take his weight.

The old guy with the faded track pants and the sunhat was tottering back and forth across the far end of the park when we emerged from the bush. He waved to us, then carried on tottering. That was the first time he'd ever acknowledged our existence! I guess he must have been a rugby league fan too.

Henry was stunned. 'This place is amazing! Wow! A Hawker Hurricane!'

'We call that the Spitfire,' I said.

'Sure,' Henry said, not asking why.

The sun was high but filtered through a streaky, grey cloud that corrugated the sky. Every now and then a frosting of tiny raindrops dampened our hair, but not our spirits, and we quickly dried off again.

For the next three hours Henry was a kid again. He ran around the fort with us as we beat off vicious attacks by a band of marauding Indians. He drove the tractor in the Indi-Tractor-poulis 500, shouting at the other tractor drivers to get out of the way.

He even squeezed into the cockpit of the Spitfire and became a World War II fighter ace, Henry the Black Knight, scourge of the Luftwaffe.

Eventually, though, he looked at his watch, and at that moment he grew eighteen years older in front of our eyes.

'Flea, Jason, it's been great,' he said. 'But I've got places to be. Jason, I'll see you around. Flea, I'll catch up with you in the pre-season training.'

I shook my head. 'I quit.'

'You quit!!' Jason and Henry said in unison.

'I already told Frank. He was OK about it.'

'Have you had an offer from another team and haven't told me about it?' Henry glared at me.

'Sort of,' I said.

'Who? The Broncos? The Knights? Not the Machetes I hope!'

I laughed. 'No. None of those. It's the Glenfield Giants. I'm kind of hoping they'll let me try out for next season.'

Henry was silent for a moment. 'That's a shame.' He checked his watch again and stood up. 'I'd better get going. Still …'

He stood there next to the Spitfire for a moment without saying anything. We both looked up at him. A giant of a man with the heart of a kid. The sun chose that moment to break through the cloud cover and its warmth washed over us, despite the cool breeze. A flock of birds whirled above the park, swooping and circling around the trees.

'Still … I'm sure we'll find plenty of time to hang out. In between my training, and your school and the Giants.'

'Absolutely,' I said with conviction. 'Absolutely.'

Henry smiled a small, sad smile as he ambled away towards the secret path. He looked back once, waved, and disappeared into the bush.

'Why'd you do it?' Jason asked after a while. 'Why'd you quit the Warriors?'

I said, 'Seems to me that I'm going to have plenty of time to be a grown-up later on. The rest of my life in fact. But I've only got this one shot at being a kid. Better make the most of it.'

'I see,' he said, although I don't really think he did. 'Sorry about calling you a smart fart, eh.'

I looked over at him. 'If your best friend can't be honest with you, then who the heck can?'

'Don't be such a gazoo,' said Jason, who said things like that. 'Guys don't have best friends. That's for girls.'

'I know.'

In the distance beyond Manuka Park I heard Henry's car start up in the car park.

We won the junior league championship the next year. And, although the Thing had come back to me a couple of days after the NRL Grand Final, I never once used it for Glenfield. It didn't seem fair.

Jenny and Phil hit it off real well and they're still together. Jenny and I are good friends though, and Phil and I can stand each other. Just.

As for the Warriors, they successfully defended their title the next season, which was also Henry's last year with the club. Thirty-two is retirement age for a rugby league player.

One day I might like to have another try-out for them.

But in the meantime, I thought I'd really, really like to play baseball for the New York Yankees ...